FTBK

P9-BYO-102

PRAISE FOR THE BAKER'S TREAT MYSTERIES

Gluten for Punishment

"Nancy J. Parra has whipped up a sweet treat that's sure to delight!"

> —Peg Cochran, national bestselling author of
> the Gourmet De-Lite Mysteries

"A delightful heroine, cherry-filled plot twists, and cream-filled pastries. Could murder be any sweeter?"

> —Connie Archer, national bestselling author of
> the Soup Lover's Mysteries

"A mouthwatering debut with a plucky protagonist. Clever, original, and appealing, with gluten-free recipes to die for."

> —Carolyn Hart, national bestselling author of
> *Death at the Door*

"A lively, sassy heroine and a perceptive and humorous look at small-town Kansas (the Wheat State)!"

> —JoAnna Carl, national bestselling author of
> the Chocoholic Mysteries

"This baker's treat rises to the occasion. Whether you need to eat allergy-free or not, you'll devour every morsel."

> —Avery Aames, Agatha Award–winning author of
> the Cheese Shop Mysteries

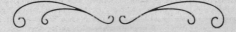

Engaged in Murder

NANCY J. PARRA

BERKLEY PRIME CRIME, NEW YORK

THE BERKLEY PUBLISHING GROUP
Published by the Penguin Group
Penguin Group (USA) LLC
375 Hudson Street, New York, New York 10014

USA • Canada • UK • Ireland • Australia • New Zealand • India • South Africa • China

penguin.com

A Penguin Random House Company

ENGAGED IN MURDER

A Berkley Prime Crime Book / published by arrangement with the author

Berkley Prime Crime Books are published by The Berkley Publishing Group.
BERKLEY® PRIME CRIME and the PRIME CRIME logo are trademarks of
Penguin Group (USA) LLC.

For information, address: The Berkley Publishing Group,
a division of Penguin Group (USA) LLC,
375 Hudson Street, New York, New York 10014.

ISBN: 978-0-425-27035-6

PUBLISHING HISTORY
Berkley Prime Crime mass-market edition / June 2014

PRINTED IN THE UNITED STATES OF AMERICA

10 9 8 7 6 5 4 3 2 1

Cover illustration by Ben Perini.
Cover design by George Long.
Interior text design by Laura K. Corless.

Chapter 1

I try to be perfect. Really, I do. In fact, I absolutely believe I could be perfect if things didn't have a way of getting between me and my ideal self. Perfectly Proper Pepper Pomeroy—that's what they called me in school. I was quite proud of the nickname until I realized that they were poking fun at me. You see, try as I may, I'm neither perfect nor proper. My hair is far too red and frizzy. I'm a tad too tall and too skinny. Not thin enough to be a supermodel and not curvy enough to catch a man's eye.

Unlike my baby sister, Felicity, who is blond, petite, and curvy in all the right places. She caught Warren Evans's eye from the moment they met at a walkathon to raise money for Lurie Children's Hospital. The two had been dating ever since, and Warren was serious. Serious enough to beg, plead, and cajole me into helping him create the perfect marriage proposal.

"You know Felicity best," he pointed out. "At least when it comes to things like her dream proposal. I want this to be something she'll always remember. I know you can see that it is."

He was right, of course. A girl never told the man she loved about her dream proposal. I mean if he really knew her, then he'd know just what to do. Right? Except men didn't know, poor slobs. So for my baby sister I planned to create a scene that was intimate, joyful, and personalized. What she always dreamed of when she dreamed of the day her Prince Charming proposed.

Besides, I liked Warren. He seemed like a great guy, and when he was with Felicity . . . well, let's say he looked at her like no man has ever looked at me.

When he asked me to help him, how could I refuse? This was my baby sister we were talking about. If I had a chance to make her happy, I wasn't going to say no. Besides, I was currently unemployed, and coming up with things for the proposal gave me something to think about besides the fact that I was perilously close to being broke—the kind of broke that meant moving back in with my parents.

I was thirty years old. The last thing I wanted was to admit defeat and move back into my old bedroom. Besides, Mom used it for her belly dancing room. Trust me, you didn't want to bunk in there, especially while she practiced.

Warren wanted to whisk Felicity away on an exotic weekend. He'd rented a private plane and asked me to create a special atmosphere inside. It'd taken some thinking, but I'd managed to design some really good decorations. I had pictures blown-up from Felicity's Facebook page. Warren had given me one he'd snapped on their first date near the Lake Michigan waterfront. Then there was the photo they had taken of them both leaping on the skydeck windows in Willis Tower. The all-glass enclosure made it look like they were flying over the city hand in hand. It was one of my favorites.

I pulled up to the tiny Executive Airport off Milwaukee Avenue in the northern suburbs of Chicago. The place was mostly used by businesses for their corporate jets to avoid the traffic in and around O'Hare or Midway. I'd been by the airport many times, but I'd never actually entered its grounds. Now my backseat was full of decorations and the twin palm plants I'd bought. The plants blocked most of my view, so I had to wing it.

I drove into the entrance, stopped at the security shack, and rolled down my car window. Yes, I had to hand crank it because my car was my Grandma Mary's and was nearly twenty years old. The Oldsmobile still ran smooth as butter even if it was big enough to rival the yachts out in the Chicago Harbor.

"Can I help you?" The guard was a young guy who looked bored out of his mind.

"I'm looking for hangar number four. I'm supposed to decorate a plane."

He squinted his blue eyes at me. A lock of blond hair fell in front of his face, and he forced it back. "You need to what?"

"Decorate a plane." I pointed my thumb at my full backseat. "It's for Warren Evans."

"You can't decorate a plane." He sounded as if he were talking to a small child. "They need to be aerodynamic to leave the ground."

"Oh, no, no, you're misunderstanding. I'm decorating the inside of a plane."

"Don't make no sense," he muttered and eyeballed the two potted palms. "Do you have any idea how big the inside of a plane is? I mean, we don't have no seven-forty-sevens taking off from this airport."

"Look, call Warren Evans. He'll straighten everything out."

"Hold on." The kid whose shirt had JIMMY embroidered above the pocket closed his window and made a phone call. He glanced at me twice as if I were a terrorist of some sort. I drummed my fingers on the steering wheel and tried not to look at the dashboard clock. The last thing I wanted was to be late and ruin Felicity's proposal.

A big man in a khaki uniform stepped out from behind the hut and leaned into my car window. "Good afternoon, miss. I'm Jeb Donaldson, airport security chief. I need to see some ID, please."

"I'm Pepper Pomeroy. I'm supposed to be at hangar number four. Warren Evans asked me to decorate a plane." I pulled out my wallet and showed him my driver's license. Why was it that whenever I had to face an officer of the law, or in this case security, I got nervous? Then to make matters worse, anytime I got nervous, I tended to talk too much. "He's going to propose to my little sister and he asked me to decorate the interior of the jet he rented. As you can see, I have several mementoes in my backseat." I pointed over my shoulder and then looked up at him with what I hoped were innocent eyes. Which I didn't need because I was innocent, but I did it anyway.

Jeb did not seem too impressed. The man had a square jaw, a full mouth, and a straight nose. His brown eyes appeared skeptical under bushy eyebrows. His hair was cut very close to the sides and flat on top. Maybe he was ex-military. He certainly had the bearing for it.

"Mr. Evans is on the phone, boss." The young security man popped his head out of the shack and handed the security chief a phone receiver.

The muscular man took it and listened while he eyed my license and then me. "I see," he said. "Yes, sir, we'll get her there." He handed the phone back to Jimmy and turned to me.

I reached out for my license. After all, he couldn't keep it hostage, could he? My fingers sort of fluttered close to him as he inspected the card.

"This card is expired."

"No, it's not," I retorted. He turned his flat stare back on me and I swallowed, hard. "Um, the sticker on the back shows it's good for another four years. See, if you have a good driving record, they merely send you a sticker when you pay to renew. That way you don't have to go down to the DMV and wait for hours. So see, it's fine. Turn it over. You'll see the sticker." I forced myself to shut up. It meant I had to bite the inside of my cheek, but I knew I had to be quiet. I had a feeling all my talking only made things worse.

He did not fill the awkward silence. It seemed he was content to draw it out as long as possible. I waited and tried to remember to breathe. It was important that I get inside the airport and to the hangar in enough time to decorate and hide before Felicity got there.

Finally, the security chief handed me back my ID.

"Hangar four is down this drive and then to your right. You'll see the numbers on top. Step inside the door and wait for Daniel Frasier, he's the pilot, or Laura Snow, she's the flight attendant." He raised his right eyebrow and studied me. "Don't go looking around unescorted or I'll have you kicked out as a safety and security risk."

"Yes, sir." I stuffed my ID back into my purse, rolled up my window, and eased through the security gate. Finding hangar number four was easy since there were only six hangars in the airport. I parked as close as possible, unlocked my car doors, and grabbed two huge bags of decorations and one of the potted palms.

The plants were bigger than I'd thought in the store, and I struggled as I tried to position the palm so that I could see around the fronds and not stumble through the door of the hangar.

"Do you need some help?" A deep baritone voice came

from the general direction of the door. I hitched the tote up on my shoulder and peered through the fronds.

"Yes, I was told to ask for Daniel Frasier or Laura Snow. I'm here to decorate a plane for Warren Evans." The last few words rose up in tone. The plant was so big and unwieldy that it was all I could do not to drop it.

"Here, let me help you with that." Two large square hands grasped the handles of the black plastic bucket I had repotted the palm in to make it easier to move. Once I was free of the plant, I could see that those hands and that voice belonged to a six-foot-tall, wide-shouldered hunk of a man with green eyes and caramel-colored hair. "I'm Daniel Frasier."

"Oh, hello," I managed to squeak out as he held the door open with his foot and handled the palm with the ease of a man who lifted heavier items on a regular basis.

"I take it you're working for Mr. Evans?"

"What? Oh, no." I adjusted the strap on the tote. "He's going to propose to my sister and he asked me to decorate his plane for their big trip this weekend." I leaned in toward him. He smelled good. You know, like a man who wears the perfect amount of expensive cologne. He wore tan flight pants and a tan buttoned shirt with shoulder flaps that held stripes to show rank of some sort. When I realized that I had quit talking and begun staring, I leaned back. "That's why I've got these decorations."

The pilot's green eyes twinkled. "I know. Come on in, I'll show you around the plane."

"Great." I followed him through the door. His backside

was as nice as his front side. Inside the hangar was dim. Large lights hung from the ceiling near the sides. Above them were skylights that let the sunlight in during the day. By now the sun had faded, leaving the large hanging lights to fill in the darkness. The space smelled of dust and grease and what I assumed was jet fuel.

"The plane is over here." He carried the plant toward one of two airplanes in the hangar. The one he walked toward was a sleek jet painted white with a blue stripe along the side. The stairs were down, allowing us access to the inside. "Watch your head as you enter."

I followed his lovely backside up and into the plane. Warren had clearly gone all out in renting a private jet. Standing in the service area was a pretty, petite brunette with blue eyes and a blue uniform. "Welcome aboard," she said in that perfect tone trained flight attendants used.

"Oh, hi," I muttered. "I'm not flying tonight. I'm only here to decorate." I lifted the bags in my hands as if I had to prove my point.

"I know," the attendant said. "I'm Laura Snow." She held out her well-groomed hand. I fumbled the bags until I got them both in one hand, reached to take her hand, and noticed that dirt had somehow gotten from the potted plant to my fingers.

"Sorry," I sighed and sort of waved at her outstretched fingers. "I'm Pepper Pomeroy."

"Don't worry, Pepper, we've been expecting you." She pulled her hand back and smiled as if she were in a tooth-paste advertisement. Yes, her teeth were gleaming white and super straight. I all but expected her to run her tongue over them to prove they were clean.

"Where do you want the palm?" Daniel asked as he did a little circle of the interior of the plane, drawing my attention. The inside of the jet had polished wood and chrome accents. A butter yellow leather couch in the rear was tucked between a door for what I assumed was a bathroom and a complete entertainment unit with movie screen and game console. The jet had a thick blue carpet and portal windows trimmed in chrome. There were two wide darker brown leather seats that faced each other between an intimate table of polished wood. I imagined it covered in a crisp white cloth and personalized with my grandmother's china. "Pepper? Where do you want the palm?"

Daniel's inquiry brought me back to the problem at hand. It seemed I had sadly overestimated the size of the aircraft. There was no way two palms were going to fit inside. Well, that was fine. One would do. "Put it in the corner behind that captain's chair." I pointed to the spot between the dark leather chair back and the small bathroom door.

Daniel placed the plant, and I set down my bags of decorations. Laura put a soft hand on my forearm.

"I'm going to step out for a bit. Let me know if you need anything."

"I'm pretty sure I have everything I need." I circled my hands over the bags. "In fact, I probably have too much, but it's always better to have too much of something than to run out, right?"

"Right." She stepped out, leaving me with Daniel and a couch that looked so soft I wanted to sit on it and see.

"How about I show you around?" Daniel offered. "It might help you get a better idea how to decorate." His green eyes sparkled, and I glanced at my watch. I might be cutting it close, but he was right. It wouldn't hurt to have a look around before I figured out where to put things. Still I needed enough time left over to do a final edit. "Always take away one item" was the rule of thumb. It had served me well so far. I wasn't about to stop now.

"That would be great as long as it doesn't take too long."

"Oh, trust me, I can be quick when I need to be." He winked.

I felt the heat of a blush rush up my neck and into my cheeks. Being a redhead, I couldn't hide a blush if I tried. I did my best to ignore the fact that my cheeks had to be as red as my hair. "I bet you can," I muttered and followed him around the interior.

Daniel pointed out the features of the fuselage, then walked back toward the cockpit. "Here is the service area where Laura will make dinner and store the champagne and coffee. In here is where I'll be." He opened a door and waved at the tiny space full of instruments. The large windows reminded me of a minivan. The actual pilot's seat appeared to be far less comfortable than the ones in the back, but then I suppose that is all part of the job.

"Nice."

He sent me a sideways grin. "I know. I fold myself up inside every time I fly, but I love the open air." He waved me toward the door and the gangway stairs. "Let's take a quick tour of the hangar so you know where the important things are, like the bathroom and how to stay safe. We wouldn't want you walking too close to the jet engines when we fire them up during our preflight test."

My eyes grew wide at the thought of accidentally being sucked into an engine. "Probably a good idea," I said and rushed by him on my way down the small set of stairs. Warren walked into the hangar as Daniel stepped down.

"Hi, Daniel." Warren strode over to us. I was so happy for Felicity. Warren was a lovely man, over six feet tall and even fitter than the pilot. Today he wore what I considered the work suit of your average accountant—a starched white shirt, black slacks, thin red tie, and a currently unbuttoned matching black suit coat. His shoes were always polished and his nails buffed. I could admire a man who knew how to pay attention to detail and still be all male.

I think Felicity loved him for his warmth, straight teeth, and the small crinkles around his dark brown eyes. Warren was the epitome of tall, dark, and handsome. Yes, my sister had every reason to gush over him.

In high school my boyfriend, Bobby, had that tall, dark, and handsome thing going for him. I remember how he used to smuggle small presents into school for me—a flower, a stuffed animal he'd won from one of those claw machines, or something as sweet as a candy kiss. It had been a while since he'd brought me gifts. I may have forgotten how to gush.

"Pepper, thanks for doing this." Warren's words pulled me from my thoughts as he brushed a dark brown hair out of his eyes.

"Have you heard from Felicity yet?" I asked.

"Yes, she called to let me know she left work and would be here in about thirty minutes."

"That doesn't give me much time." I worried my bottom lip. "Daniel needs to show me the safe areas of the hangar and where the bathrooms are so I can hide without getting hurt. Oh, did you give the gate guy Cesar's name?"

"Cesar?"

"Yes, the videographer I hired to film the entire thing."

"Is he going to film inside the plane?"

I glanced over at the plane, thought through the small interior, and winced. "Yes?"

"No worries," Daniel said. "I know right where to stash a body, er . . . I mean man with a camera."

"Really?" I tilted my head, trying to decide if he was kidding or not.

"Really." Daniel winked at me and I decided he was teasing.

Warren nodded. A look passed between the men, and Daniel took me by the arm. "Come on, I'll show you around."

"Wait!" I turned my head back to Warren. "Felicity still thinks that your car is busted and you need a ride, right? I mean, you don't think she suspects anything, do you?"

"I don't think she suspects anything," Warren reassured me. "Go, your time is running out."

I let Daniel take me away from Warren. "I'm not used to being in a hangar. It's not like I have my own airplane. Please be specific on the safety stuff. I'm a bit of a klutz and I don't want to spoil Felicity's surprise by accident."

"Don't worry, I'll be specific." He pointed out the thick heavy pods under each wing. "Those are the engines. You'll be safe if you stay in the front of the plane." He walked me around the nose. "So from the stairs to about here." He stopped at the edge of the plane's window on the side opposite the stairs.

"What about that door back there?" I asked as I craned my neck to peer down the length of the plane. "Why would they put a door in the danger zone?"

Daniel laughed, showing white teeth. "That's for the pros. Trust me, you don't need to go any farther than I showed you."

"The bathrooms must be over here, then?" I waved at the cinder block area near the mouth of the hangar. It was almost straight across from the plane's window. Which meant it was in the safe zone.

"That's right, smart girl." He took my elbow and led me back toward the steps and the interior of the plane. "Now, let's go inside and I'll show you where to hide your videographer."

I paused and batted my lashes at him. "Is that a line?"

13

He tilted his head. "Why, Miss Pomeroy, whatever do you mean?"

"It sort of sounded like you were asking me inside to look at your sketches."

He laughed and waggled his eyebrows. "Maybe I was. Why don't you come in and see?"

This time I laughed as well. "Thank you for the invitation, but I have a boyfriend. Besides I really have to get to work. My sister will be here in twenty-five minutes."

"No harm done, I hope." He raised both hands in innocent defeat. "I'll show you where to hide a man and let you get to it."

I shook my head at his double entendre and followed him up the stairs. As he touched the railing, I noticed the wedding ring on his finger and shook my head. My boyfriend, Bobby, wasn't the greatest guy, but at least his presence kept the married flirts an arm's distance from me.

Chapter 2

"You want to put the videographer where?"

"The toilet is perfect," Daniel insisted. "He can set up his camera here." He patted the built-in end table beside the couch. "Then he can stow himself in here until after Mr. Ev—I mean, Warren, proposes."

I peered into the bathroom. It was twice the size of a normal plane toilet. The fixtures were sumptuous yet efficient. "Is it safe?"

"Safer than standing behind the potted plant." Daniel pointed at my palm tree. He did have a point.

"Maybe if I brought in the second palm . . ."

"Don't you think that would look really suspicious?"

I tightened my lips and raised a corner of my mouth.

"No more suspicious than having him hide behind red velvet curtains with only his shoes showing."

He looked at me with drawn together eyebrows. "There aren't any curtains on board . . ."

"Inspector Clouseau?"

"Who?"

"Pink Panther movies?"

"I've never heard of them . . ."

"Oh, well, then we can't be friends," I said. "If you don't know the movies where the assistant/butler jumps out and tries to kill the inspector, you'll never get my sense of humor."

"Oh, I get your sense of humor." There was a smile in his eye that warmed my heart.

I held out my hand like a stop sign. "Fine, we'll put Cesar in the toilet. Thanks for your help, but I can take it from here."

"Are you sure?"

"I'm sure." I gave him my best smile and looked knowingly from his wedding ring back to his face. I think he blushed a bit or maybe I'd like to think he blushed. Either way he was nearly to the door before I remembered that I needed to chill the champagne. "Wait!"

He turned, his eyes wide and eyebrows up.

"I forgot to ask where the mini fridge is." I held up the champagne and bakery box filled with my sister's favorite mini cream puffs.

"Sure you did." He gave me a slow wink. "You'll find the mini fridge built in beside the couch." He pointed behind me to the table where we planned to stash the hidden camera. "If you think of anything else you need, I'll be right outside."

"No, I've got it from here, thanks." I waved him off and told myself not to admire his backside. Time was running out. I found the handle on the end table and opened it. Daniel hadn't lied. This really was a mini fridge. Popping the things that needed to be cool inside, I quickly unpacked the bags I'd dragged in.

I placed a conch shell on the table with a replica of the lei Felicity had worn when they took a trip to Hawaii. It had taken them a full year to save up for that trip, but it was all Felicity talked about. Then there were the posters of the picnic in Grant Park, where they had had their second date. I put a video from the comedy club where they hung out on Friday nights into the plane's DVR.

By the time I was done, the place was tastefully decorated to reflect the timeline of Felicity and Warren's dating history. I had done a bang-up job, if I had to say so myself, and I did since no one else was around.

I glanced at my watch. The videographer had to be here soon if he was going to get candid shots of Felicity coming in and then hide in the bathroom to await the big moment when Warren popped the question.

The air smelled of sunset and wine, Felicity's treasured candles. The soft sounds of the couple's favorite band played through the sound system. I loved to plan parties. In fact, Mom always said I had thrown my first party at the age of three, complete with hand-picked wildflowers beside my pretend tea and crumbling cookies. It had been so much fun that I had made my baby sister sit through event after carefully planned event our entire childhood.

Mom liked to say I went overboard, but then again she always knew she could count on me when she needed something important planned. It didn't matter how busy I was. I loved to come to the rescue and coordinate the event.

I sighed at the perfection in front of me, making sure that it pleased all the senses. There was a banging near the door and I realized the time. I gathered up the remaining bags and wadded them all into one. I then adjusted the silver metal ice bucket, took one last look, and exited the plane.

Warren and Daniel chatted about flight details. I scooted around the front of the plane in the safety zone as the cameraman entered the building. Happy to see he was on time, I rushed to him. "Cesar! I'm so glad you're here. You had me worried."

"I'm so sorry. I got stuck in traffic. There was some kind of accident on the Stevenson. Then the guy at the gate had to check my ID."

"You're here now. Let me show you what to do inside the plane and then, if there is time, you can take some candid shots as my sister arrives."

"Sure thing." His dark brown eyes glittered in the light. Cesar was a young guy I'd met a few months ago at a family event. He'd filmed my cousin's wedding and the video was edited so well I knew I had to have him for Felicity's proposal.

I took his smallest case from him and put my arm through his. "Come on. She could be here any moment." Cesar was about five feet nine inches tall and slender. His light brown skin and soft black hair spoke of his Latin heritage. His camera bag was bigger than the overnight case I'd packed for Felicity, which spoke of his true love—film. He wore jeans and a dark blue T-shirt underneath a dark green, long-sleeved shirt.

The plan was for Cesar to tape until Warren popped the question, then depart before the flight took off to whatever secret destination Warren had planned for the weekend. It was all hush-hush. But I deduced that it was somewhere warm yet upscale since Warren had asked me to pack Felicity's swimsuit and a cocktail dress.

Once I got Cesar all squared away, I exited the plane in search of the flight attendant. It never hurt to give a few tips on how to serve the champagne and the treats I had stowed away in the service area of the plane.

I was careful to go around the front of the plane and avoid the engines. Daniel was in the cockpit working on his preflight checks. It was best to stay in the safety zone, where he could see me. He looked up and we locked gazes. He winked and I blushed and scurried toward the restrooms. Thank goodness Laura was no longer at the back of the plane. I didn't want to have to make either one of us cross in front of the engines.

The rest of the hangar was empty so I figured she was in the ladies' room. I know it's where I would be before a flight. I hurried down the tiny cinder block hallway and knocked on the door. When no one answered, I grabbed the handle and turned. It opened with ease. "Laura? It's me, Pepper. I need to give you a few last-minute tips. Laura?"

I thought I heard a noise so I stepped farther inside the room. It was all tile with three stalls and three sinks. The lights were fluorescent and buzzed, then dimmed and brightened in random patterns. A glance in the mirror told me that my hair had frizzed up in the humidity. I tried to plaster it down. The last thing I wanted was to look embarrassingly unkempt whenever Felicity showed people the video of her big moment.

The room was quiet except for the buzzing. I ducked down to see if there were any feet showing under the stall. "Laura?" Two of the stalls had nothing. The third stall was blocked by what looked like feet, except they were large like a man's and pointed the wrong direction.

Of course I never believe anything that seems oddly out of place unless I double-check it. "Laura?" I pushed on the stall door and it knocked halfway open. Something large and firm was inside the stall between me and the wall.

It wasn't easy but I squeezed my head and shoulders through the opening to get a better look. It was the third stall and outfitted for the disabled so it was two and a half times the size of the other two stalls. That way a person could get a wheelchair in and out of it with ease.

Instead of a wheelchair, there was a large metal bucket with a mop sticking out between me and the rest of the space. The air in the stall smelled of pine-scented cleaner, most likely from the mop. Clearly it wasn't Laura in the stall. How did I explain the shoes I thought I saw? I wrestled the mop and bucket out of the way and saw what looked like a pile of men's clothing until I got to the brown hair sticking through.

Startled, I might have screamed a little. Then things became a bit of a blur as my heart raced and my adrenaline kicked in. "You can't be in here!" I was firm and yanked the brown suit coat off the man's face. He didn't respond.

The guy was too well dressed to be homeless. He was fully clothed in a blue shirt and brown slacks and wedged up in the corner half on and mostly off the toilet seat. His limp hand hung down into the toilet water. His head rested against the wall, his mouth slack-jawed.

I'd seen passed-out guys before, but none of them had gone out this much. Should I shake him? Wake him and force him out?

I glanced at his feet. He was large, and if I got too forceful, he might wake up a mad and crazy drunk. My wild imagination had him backhanding me by accident, knocking me against the wall. The last thing I wanted was to get accidentally beaten up by a drunk moments before Felicity's proposal.

"Hello? Um, wake up!" My words echoed through the bathroom or at least I think they echoed. Maybe my thoughts echoed. I mean, how close could you get to a guy who was passed out without getting hurt?

I realized I had the mop beside me. It would make a good weapon and a good poker. I yanked it out of the bucket, not surprised that the noise didn't wake this guy. At this point I figured he was probably deaf, which meant no matter how loudly I yelled, he would sleep on.

So instead of yelling, I poked him on the shoulder with the mop handle. "Hey, mister, wake up. You can't be in here."

It was then someone decided it was a good idea to pound on the bathroom door. I jumped, startled, and screamed, turning the mop handle toward the door. "What?"

"Hey, Pepper, get out here. Felicity's at the gate." Warren's voice shot through my shock.

"Coming!" All my thoughts turned to my sister and her impending proposal. I stepped out of the stall and away from the strange drunk inside it. The mop went back into the bucket and I pushed it out of the way in case the drunk decided to leave on his own.

One glance back at the man and I had to wonder. Should I say something and ruin Felicity's big moment, or should I wait until my sister said yes before I mention the drunken man in the ladies' room?

Chapter 3

Of course, I could call the cops on the drunk. But as I stood in the hallway with my cell phone in hand, I saw my lovely sister rush into the hangar. She looked flushed with excitement. Her long hair gleamed in the sunset. She wore a navy suit, which consisted of a navy pencil skirt and matching jacket with three-quarter-length sleeves. On her left wrist sparkled the diamond bracelet Warren had given her for Christmas the year before. She wore navy and white spectator pumps that showed off her legs.

Felicity gave Warren a kiss on the mouth hello. He dipped her and my heart stopped. It was a real-life movie moment. How could I spoil it with police cars and questions?

I glanced at the bathroom door. The drunk guy,

whoever he was, wasn't going anywhere. I decided right then and there to wait until after Felicity said yes and Warren whisked her away. After all, what could it hurt? No one would ever know but me, and even better, the guy might wake up and leave while Warren proposed. Then I wouldn't have to call anyone.

A movement on the right caught my eye, and a jolt of fear went through me. Was the drunk man going to wake up and spoil Felicity's moment? A second later I was relieved to identify the movement as the flight attendant, Laura. She nodded at me and put her finger to her lips as Felicity's voice drifted into range.

"Warren, are you okay?" Felicity placed her hands on either side of his face and studied him.

"Yes, of course," he replied with a smile. "Come on." He took her hand and wrapped it in the crook of his arm. "Let's go inside. You can meet my friend Daniel and check out his plane."

"Are you going to tell me why I'm here?" Felicity asked as he helped her up the gangway.

"I'm working on Daniel's accounts. Once I'm done, we can go to dinner." Warren told the lie smoothly. The thought crossed my mind that he lied almost too smoothly—as if he had a lot of practice. Laura and I waited just out of sight until Felicity and Warren disappeared into the jet. Then I caught a tear in Laura's eye at the romance of the moment, and I found myself crossing into the hangar without another thought.

I ducked under the nose of the plane and glanced above

it to see Daniel give a thumbs-up. I suddenly heard a squeal come from inside the plane, and I could picture Felicity throwing herself into Warren's arms.

Daniel stuck his head out of the plane. "Come on in, guys. She said yes!!"

My heart leapt for the second time in a matter of minutes. This time for joy, rather than terror. I put the face of the drunk out of my head as I climbed into the plane.

Felicity and Warren sat on the soft leather couch. Laura poured champagne in thin flutes and passed the crystal glasses to the happy couple. Then she gave one to me and one to Daniel. I glanced at him. "Are you supposed to drink and fly?" I asked, cocking an eyebrow.

"Your sister will be safe," he assured me. "I'll only take a sip for good luck." He raised his glass. "To the happy couple!"

"To the happy couple!" we all repeated and I took a sip of the champagne.

"You knew about this all along, didn't you?" Felicity pointed her finger at me.

I smiled and shrugged. "Maybe . . ."

"Pepper planned the entire thing." Warren raised his glass to me in a mini toast. "Your sister is a gem."

Felicity got up and flung her arms around me and hugged me tightly. "Thank you! This is the best proposal setting ever."

I hugged her back. "I'm so glad you think so. I wanted it to be perfect for you."

She kissed my cheek. "It's perfect." Her beautiful blue eyes sparkled with tears of joy. "Thank you!"

Warren came over and wrapped his arm around her waist. "Yes, Pepper, thank you. You made us both very happy people."

A tear formed in my eye as warmth spread through my heart. I dashed the tear away with a finger and raised my glass. "To a lifetime of joy for Felicity and Warren."

Everyone toasted again.

"Oh, no, you don't," Laura said with a laugh as she snatched the glass out of Daniel's hand. "We still have a plane to fly."

"Fly?" Felicity looked up at Warren. "You mean we're really going somewhere? But I don't have anything packed."

"Don't worry, Pepper packed for you." Warren nodded at me.

"Pepper?"

"I raided your closet," I admitted. "Oh, and we got the entire proposal on tape. Cesar, come on out."

I waved at the bathroom door and Cesar popped out with the camera on his shoulder. The light was a bit blinding.

"You taped the whole thing?" Felicity clapped her hand over her mouth.

I froze. Was she happy or sad? "Yes?"

"Oh, how wonderful!" She flung her arms around my neck for the second time, spilling champagne on my blouse. "Thank you, thank you!"

"My pleasure." I hugged her back.

"Okay, all ashore who are going ashore," Daniel said and waved toward the open door. He glanced at his watch. "We have ten minutes to get her rolling and taxi up to our flight plan."

"Where are we going?" Felicity asked me.

"That is top secret, my love." Warren took her hand in his and kissed her fingers. "Go sit down and get comfortable. I'll see Cesar and Pepper out."

"Congratulations!" I said as I followed Cesar to the door. The cameraman turned off his light and ducked his head as he stepped down the small gangway.

"Pepper." Warren touched my shoulder. I turned to him. "I can never thank you enough. Everything was perfect." He hugged me.

"It was my pleasure." I patted him on the back and felt him slip something into my pocket. Drawing back, I reached inside and felt the distinctive paper of a check. I frowned. "You already reimbursed me for all my expenses."

He grabbed my hand, enveloped it between both of his in a warm embrace. "It's the least I could do. I hope you realize that there are a lot of people who would pay big bucks for help like this. You're a natural. You know how to make things special."

The heat of a blush rushed up my cheeks. "It's a fun hobby."

"It shouldn't be." He gave me a sincere look.

"Let's go, kids, time's a wastin'," Daniel said over his shoulder as he flipped switches.

The last thing I wanted was to be caught near the plane when the engines kicked in. "Take care of my sister," I said.

"I will," Warren said. "Don't worry. I have a few more surprises for her." He winked and the next thing I knew I was off the plane, standing with my back against the cinder block hallway. Felicity peered out the window and waved. I waved back. She looked so happy. Her joy brought tears to my eyes.

I waved until they taxied out of sight. Stepping out of the hangar, I watched as the plane started down the runway. In a moment it was gently lifting into the sky. Daniel circled the airport, dipping his wing before he took off for parts unknown.

I shaded my eyes from the sun and waved like a madwoman. Felicity was a very lucky girl. Then I remembered the check Warren had slipped into my pocket. I pulled it out and stared at it. What? Who writes a check for so much money? I blinked at all the zeros.

The words "think about making this a career" were written in a manly scrawl on the memo line of the check. "If I could make this much money planning proposals, I'm all over it," I muttered. Seriously, this check would go a long way toward paying off my bills. I decided I liked Warren more and more.

Funny, seeing such a large sum on a check was so strange, I couldn't wrap my brain around it.

It usually took a lot to throw me off my game, but a check this size immediately following finding a guy in the ladies' room . . . well, I'd have to say those were two of the biggest shocks of my life within an hour's time frame. Wait! Crap, how could I forget the drunk guy in the ladies' room?

I shoved the check deep into the pocket of my skinny jeans and dialed 911 on my cell phone.

"Emergency Dispatch," a woman said in a monotone voice. "What is your emergency?"

"Yes, hi, I'm Pepper Pomeroy and I need to report a drunk guy in the third stall of the ladies' room."

"And that is an emergency because?"

"He's drunk—passed out—incapacitated . . . in the ladies' room. Please send someone out to take care of him."

"What is your current address?" the dispatch operator asked.

"I'm at the Executive Airport, hangar number four."

"Are you hurt?"

"No, I'm fine."

"Did you try to rouse him?"

My thoughts went back to the poke in the shoulder with the mop handle. "Yes . . . He didn't wake up."

"Did you call airport security?"

"No, but that's a good idea. Are you going to send out a police car?"

"It's standard procedure when someone calls," the operator said. Her voice was calm and unassuming.

"Oh, okay, good."

"Are you in any danger?"

"Not that I know of." I shrugged but then realized she was on the phone and didn't see the shrug. A quick look around and I realized that Cesar had not come back since following the jet to film the take off. "There's no one here but me."

"There's a patrol car on the way," the dispatcher said. "I would ask you to stay on the line, but since you appear to be in no danger, hang up and call airport security."

"Right, thanks," I said and hit the End button. Then I realized I didn't know the number to the airport security guys. I mean, who knows that? Then I remembered that the head of security had given me his business card when I came through the door.

Now all I had to do was find where I put it. I checked my pockets. Yeah, not there. Did I put it in my purse? I left my bag and stuff over by the hall. It occurred to me that there might be a phone in the office across from the restrooms. If there was a phone, there may be an emergency number list. That might be a better plan than searching my pockets.

I turned on the light switch. The room smelled old and mildewy. I saw a phone on the desk in the middle. Beside it was a list of extensions to call.

It seems luck was on my side. I picked up my phone and dialed the number I'd found on the desktop.

"Executive Airport, this is Jeb, how can I help you?"

"Hi, Mr. Donaldson, this is Pepper Pomeroy. I'm at hangar number four and there's a drunk guy passed out in the ladies' bathroom."

"What?"

"Don't worry, I called the police. They promised they were on their way."

"Don't touch anything." His tone was authoritative.

"I haven't," I reassured him. "At least not recently."

"I'm coming right down there." I heard a car door open and then slam closed. "Are you okay?"

"Yes, I'm fine."

"He didn't try to hit on you, did he?"

"What? No, he's passed out . . . at least he was when I was in the bathroom."

"When was that?"

"Just before Felicity and Warren took off on their flight . . ."

"So he could no longer be there."

"Oh, right. I'll go check—"

"No. Don't! Meet me at the door. Don't touch anything!"

"You already said that," I mumbled then realized there was no way he could hear me with all the noise he was making so I hung up. Okay, that question made me a little paranoid. I hadn't thought I was in any danger. I mean, he was a drunk guy, right?

Then it occurred to me that if as I previously feared, the drunk guy came to and walked out the side door there would be no drunk guy in the bathroom when the cops got here. The last thing I needed was to be hit with a fine for calling the police when it wasn't warranted.

I hurried back out. No one was in the small hallway.

I pushed open the door and stuck my head inside the bathroom. "Anyone in here?" I asked. "Mister, are you still here?" Dead silence followed.

I moved toward the stall and pushed the door open. Thankfully the drunk guy was still in the same position. "Oh, thank goodness." I put a hand on my heart. "Okay, mister, come on. Get up. I've called the police."

I pushed on his arm with the broom handle and it flopped oddly to the side. His head lolled onto his shoulder and I realized that he smelled really bad.

Narrowing my eyes in suspicion, I stepped forward. "Hey." I snapped my fingers. "Wake up. The police are on their way. Hey. Are you okay?"

Nothing.

I bit my lip as a strange feeling crawled up my spine. Was he passed out? Or was he dead?

That thought was creepy. I studied him more closely. There was a bluish tinge around his mouth. He seemed stiff. I didn't want to touch him. I really didn't. Did I mention that he smelled bad? What if he woke up? He'd scare the demons right out of me.

"You're not dead, are you?"

He didn't reply.

I straightened and put my hands on my hips. Common sense prevailed and I realized I didn't want to be alone with a possibly drunk or dead man. So I stepped out of the stall and dialed my boyfriend, Bobby, but he didn't answer and I remembered that he was at a noisy bar. He probably couldn't hear his phone.

"Leave a message at the beep and I'll get back to you as soon as I can."

Beep.

"Hi, Bobby, it's Pepper. Listen, I'm going to be late. Something has come up at the airport. Oh, ha! A pun. Get it? Something is up at an airport?" I laughed when I was nervous. I also tended to say silly things. "Anyway, I might be here a bit so go ahead and start without me."

Disappointed that I couldn't talk to him live and in person during this scary time in my life, I pressed the Off button and glanced around. The shadows lengthened and I wondered how much longer it would be before the police got here.

"Miss Pomeroy?"

I heard Jeb calling my name and ran out of the bathroom. "I'm here." I hurried forward toward the open hangar door.

The hangar door was wide-open so he could see me from one hundred feet away. He hitched his gun belt on his narrow hips as he hurried toward me. "I thought I asked you to stay outside the hangar."

"I wanted to make sure the guy was still in the ladies' room," I said. "He is, by the way."

"All right," he said. His wide shoulders and muscular biceps were reassuring. "Did you touch him?"

"No," I said and followed Jeb down the hallway. "I have to admit, I'm kind of worried that he may be more than passed out."

"What do you mean by 'more than passed out'?" He

stopped at the bathroom door and studied me with his intense brown gaze.

"I don't know." I worried my bottom lip. "He may be dead."

"You're telling me that you think the drunk in the ladies' room is dead?"

"Yes."

"Did you check for a pulse?" He pushed the door open and I followed him into the ladies' room.

"You told me not to touch him."

Jeb went straight to the third stall and looked inside. He muttered something dark under his breath and then turned on his heel. "You need to leave. This is a crime scene and I need to secure it."

I took off at the sound of his voice. He spooked me with his hand on his gun belt and his serious gaze. I was outside and beside old blue before I realized it.

The sound of an approaching police car echoed through the wide-open hangar. I waved at the car, and the inhabitants cut their sirens. The sudden loss of noise was nearly as deafening as the sirens themselves. The police car lights flashed in a rhythm that was the opposite of the security vehicle's, and the effect was rather like a disco ball.

I rushed to the two officers as they exited the cars. "Hi, I'm Pepper Pomeroy. I called 911."

The driver of the car was about six feet tall and slender. "Officer O'Riley," he said, his blue eyes solemn. "You called regarding a drunk in the ladies' room?"

"Yes, only I'm thinking he may be more than drunk."

Officer O'Riley narrowed his eyes. "What do you mean by 'more than drunk'?"

"I think he might be dead." I winced. "I'm sorry. I would have called sooner if I'd thought he was dead dead and not simply a dead drunk." Okay, so I babbled when I was scared. I shut my mouth and tried to slow my racing heart.

"How do you know he's dead?" the second officer asked.

"This is my partner, Officer Vandall," Officer O'Riley said.

"Hi." I waved then stuffed my hands in my pockets. "He didn't move when I tried to wake him. I thought he was just passed out, but he smells kind of funky and he's really stiff."

"Call in backup," O'Riley ordered his partner. "Where is he?"

"This way." I pointed down the hall. "I discovered him in the third stall of the ladies' room." I led them down the beige-painted cinder block hall. The doors were painted beige to match the walls. The only way you knew it was a door was the silver-plated handle and the little black outline of a stick figure in a skirt.

"Stay here." Officer O'Riley held up his left hand to stop my progress. His right hand was on the butt of his gun.

"Jeb Donaldson is in there," I said. "He's head of airport security."

"Did he find the body?"

"No, I did," I said. "I called him after I called 911." I wrapped my hands around my waist, leaned against the wall, and watched. There was quite a commotion when the officers entered the restroom. After a moment of chaos, Jeb was escorted out of the bathroom by Officer Vandall.

"I told you, I'm head of airport security. It's my job to make sure no one messed with the crime scene," Jeb grumbled as Officer Vandall put him against the wall beside me.

"Is this the guy you called?" the officer asked me. For a brief moment I contemplated saying no, but the look of murder in Jeb's gaze gave me pause.

"Yes," I said.

"Stay here, both of you," Officer Vandall warned. "We'll need to get your statements." He reached up on his shoulder and hit his communication device. "Dispatch, this is Unit 73. We need Crime Scene Patrol and an ambulance to the Executive Airport, hangar number four. They won't need to run with lights. There is a confirmed DB. Again DB is confirmed."

The device made a squawking noise that he seemed to understand and he turned back to us. Pulling out a notebook and a pen, he asked. "Okay, let's take it from the top. Who discovered the body?"

"I did—"

"She did—"

We answered at the same time. The officer nodded and made a note on his pad. "Ms. Pomeroy, is it?"

"Yes, sir, Pepper Pomeroy."

As he wrote down my name, a third officer came in. "What have we got?" The new guy looked more like a Boy Scout than a police officer. I looked at Officer Vandall as if to ask if this new guy was a real cop.

"We have a DB," Officer Vandall said. "This is Officer Flynn. Is Westin with you?"

"Right here," came the sound of a second male voice. Suddenly the place was full of men.

Jeb crossed his arms and leaned back against the wall. "The scene is secure," he grumbled. "I secured it."

"I'm sure you did," Officer Vandall said as the other two went into the bathroom.

A moment later, Officer Flynn came out of the restroom. He looked a little green as he rushed by.

"It's his first DB," Vandall said.

The sound of retching came from around the corner. My stomach leapt into my throat. Was it really that bad? Wait, this was my first dead body, too . . . My heartbeat picked up and my palms broke out in a sweat.

"Sit down," Officer Vandall ordered and pushed my shoulder as my knees gave out.

I sat down hard. My vision started to go dark. Great, just what I needed . . . to faint in front of the cops. It could be worse, I suppose. I could be outside with Officer Flynn. Or worse, inside marring Officer O'Riley's shiny shoes.

"Head between your knees." He put his pad away and squatted beside me. I had to admit that the ground felt particularly comfortable at the moment. I rested my forehead on the cool tiled floor.

"I'm fine," I muttered.

"I'm sure you are," he said.

Why then did I have tears in my eyes?

Chapter 4

⚥

"I have a blanket in my truck," I heard Jeb say.

"Get it." Vandall's voice was full of sympathy. "You had quite a shock, Ms. Pomeroy. Take a deep breath in and blow it out. Good."

I felt the blanket go around my shoulders. The warmth staved off the shivers that had started down my spine. I sat up to look into Vandall's hazel gaze. He had those lovely diamond-shaped eyes that were wider in the center and pointed at the ends as if he spent days laughing in the sun. "I'm fine."

"I'm going to have to ask you some more questions," he said. "Are you up to it?"

"Yes." I nodded.

"There's an office across the hall," Jeb said. "You can take her in there."

Both men helped me up and I huddled in the blanket. The office door was open and the overhead light still on from my excursion inside to find Jeb's phone number. I walked in, this time sensitive to my surroundings. The office held a file cabinet, a desk with a chair behind it, and two chairs in front.

Officer Vandall ushered me into the second chair in front of the desk. He looked at Jeb. "Can you get her some water?"

"Sure thing." Jeb left and I huddled in the blanket as Officer Vandall leaned against the desk and studied me.

"Tell me how you found the body." His hazel gaze was calm and direct.

"I looked under the stall and saw a man's feet so I knocked on the door. There was no way I was going to use the restroom if a guy was in there." I had a feeling I would get in big trouble for letting Felicity and Warren leave the scene of a crime. But I really had thought he was simply drunk. Then I'd gotten caught up in the excitement of the moment. Warren and I had worked so hard to create the perfect scene for Felicity.

Besides, favor from a friend or not, renting the plane and crew must be costing Warren a fortune. It would have been a tragedy for him to go to all that expense only to be grounded due to a crime. There was no way Warren or his crew was involved. No way.

"Let's start from the beginning." Officer Vandall pulled out his paper and pen. "Why are you here?"

"Well, you see, my mom and dad were taking this romantic vacation to—"

"At the airport, today . . ." He gave me a deadpan look. You know the kind your mom gives you when you're caught goofing around.

"Oh." I smiled. Luckily Jeb came in with a tiny paper cup filled with water. "Thank you." I took the cup from him and sipped. It was cold and sweet on my tongue and throat and gave me time to reason out my story. I would tell the truth, I decided. Well, as much of the truth as I could anyway.

"I'll need to question you separately," Officer Vandall said to Jeb. "If you don't mind . . ."

"Oh, right." Jeb shoved his hands in his pockets and left the office.

I noticed two guys in paramedic uniforms walk by the office window pushing a stretcher. They were followed by a single gentleman wearing a black jacket marked CST. He looked young, thin, and nothing like the actors on television.

"Is one guy enough to process a crime scene?" I asked.

"That's Frank Swizer. He's the best. Now let's start with why you're here in hangar four today, Ms. Pomeroy."

"I came to help my sister's boyfriend, Warren Evans, propose to my sister. You see, he wanted to give Felicity her dream proposal and I knew exactly what she always wanted." I paused, waiting for him to ask. He gave me the flat-eyed stare. "She wanted to be proposed to in a private jet and whisked away to a romantic weekend. Thus the Executive Airport." I waved my hand and sloshed the bit of water left in the paper cup.

"So you came to help this guy, Warren, propose . . ."

"Yes, no, wait . . . I didn't help him propose. I mean it's not romantic if your sister proposes for the guy. It wasn't like I put words in his mouth or anything. I came to decorate the inside of the plane with mementos of their relationship. Then there was the music and the flowers and the champagne and the chocolate-covered strawberries . . . you know."

"So when did you find the body? Before or after this Warren proposed to your sister Felicity?"

I swallowed. I was the worst liar in the world. My face heated up and I tended to stutter. "I thought he was a drunk guy . . . you know, passed out."

He glared at me as my face grew warmer. I refused to let his silence unnerve me.

"Do you really think I would have let them leave me here alone with a dead body?"

"Just a drunk guy . . ."

"As far as I knew, he might have gotten up and left while I saw Felicity off . . ." I swallowed. "He might have."

He didn't answer. Instead he wrote something in his notebook. I crossed my arms and jutted out my chin. I told myself to wait him out.

The tension in the room grew as the time stretched on. I bit down on my tongue until I tasted blood. Finally, he took pity on me and broke the silence.

"So you called immediately after their plane took off."

"Pretty much," I replied.

He raised his right eyebrow. "Why did you go into the ladies' room?"

"When I got here, Daniel, Warren's pilot, showed me around. He told me how to be safe around the plane and gave me a tour of the hangar. After I decorated the plane, I wanted to give Laura Snow—she's the flight attendant Warren used—some pointers on serving the champagne so I looked for her in the ladies' room. After the plane took off, I thought I heard someone so I went down the hall but no one was there."

"After the plane left the hangar, you didn't see anyone?"

"No, I guess I was the only one here. That's why I called 911 first to report the drunk guy. There wasn't any airport security around. After I called you, the operator suggested I call Jeb. So I did. He told me not to touch anything and came up in the truck you see there." I pointed out the office window.

"When did you figure out the victim was dead?"

"When Jeb asked me if the drunk guy was still there," I said. "I had to check. I didn't want to file a police report if he'd gotten up and left."

"So you went in and tried to wake him."

"Yes, that's when I noticed the smell and the weird stiffness and the funny blue color of his lips . . ."

"Did you check for a pulse?"

"No, I was afraid. Then Jeb came into the hangar. I told him where the body was. That's when he went inside the bathroom. He said he was a trained professional."

"And all this time you didn't see anyone else?"

"No, no, I was the only one here. Why?"

"I'm wondering where the killer was . . ."

A shiver ran down my back at the thought that I had been alone with not only a dead man but perhaps his killer. "The only one in the restroom when I found the body was me. Trust me, I checked. You see, I have this habit of looking under the stalls to see if they're empty—especially if I'm in a guy place like the mechanic's or something. It's safer. A girl never knows who might be lurking . . ."

"Or dead."

"Right." I waved my hand to emphasize my words.

"Where were you when you called 911?"

"I was in the hallway," I answered.

"Did you see anyone else?"

"No."

"Did you touch anything?"

"Well, I guess I touched the door to go in, then the stall door . . ."

"Frank will be collecting fingerprints . . ."

"I'm not lying." I could feel my face flush. Okay, so I might be fibbing about the timeline a bit, but I was being as honest as possible.

"What makes you think I would think you're lying?" He raised an eyebrow as he twisted my words.

"You are acting as if I'm a suspect." I pouted and folded my arms across my chest.

"Do you usually skip work to plan an event like this proposal?" he asked.

"No." I frowned. "I was recently laid off. They were reorganizing corporate and my job was eliminated. They said it was"—I made finger quotes—"'redundant.'"

"I see. How long ago was that?"

I frowned. "Last month." I winced at how fast time had gone by. My unemployment stipend was only two-thirds of the salary that Events Inc. had paid me as a corporate event planner. Thank goodness for Warren's check. That chunk of money would help pay my bills for a few months.

"Were you angry they let you go?" Officer Vandall asked.

I tilted my head and gave him the squinty eye. "Are you thinking I was a disgruntled employee offing my boss? Because (a) I have no idea how that man in there died, and (b) I've never seen him before in my life."

"I see," Officer Vandall said. "What about your sister?"

"What about her?" I tugged the blanket tight around my shoulders.

"Did she know the man in the bathroom?"

"How would I know?" I shrugged. "As far as I know, she didn't use the bathroom while she was here. Besides, every moment from the time she left the cab until after the proposal was filmed by my video guy. I think I would have noticed if he followed her into the restroom."

"There's video of this event?"

"Yes, of course . . ."

"I need that footage," he said. "Where's the videographer?"

"Cesar? He followed the plane out to catch a clip of it taking off into the sunset. I didn't see him come back, so I presume he headed back to his office."

"I'm going to need his information."

"Okay," I said. "I have his info in my phone." I reached into my pocket and pulled out my cell phone. Thank goodness for smart phones. I flipped through the screens until I got to Cesar's contact info, then I showed Officer Vandall the screen. "He's really good and reasonable if you ever have an event you need filmed."

"I'll keep that in mind." He wrote down Cesar's information. "Who else was here that can verify your story?"

"First of all, it's not a story. It's what happened." I narrowed my eyes at him.

He gave me that same calm stare.

"Fine, when I arrived, I met Warren at the entrance to the hangar." I waved toward what I had begun to think of as the giant garage door. "Then there was Daniel Frasier, he's the pilot. Then Laura Snow, she's the stewardess. Do they call them that anymore?" I shrugged. "That's pretty much it. Cesar came later and then Felicity."

"And you were the only one here when you found the body . . ."

"If that is a question, the answer is yes. Daniel piloted the plane. Laura ensured everyone's safety and comfort. Cesar went out to the runway to film the takeoff."

"And you were here, alone in a wide-open hangar . . ."

I winced. "Yes, is that weird? I mean, I've never been in a hangar before. I kind of thought there would be mechanics or someone else around. Ask Jeb Donaldson, he's airport security. He should know more than I do about who should be here and who shouldn't."

"Tell me more about Warren Evans," he asked as if we were getting to know each other over coffee. I didn't fall for it, though.

"He's been dating my sister for a year or so."

"Where did they meet?"

"Why is that important?"

He tilted his head. "Humor me."

"Fine." I wiggled in my plastic chair. "They met at a charity thing. Look, I really don't know him that well. I think he's an accountant for a small firm that does something for the airport. It's how he knows Daniel and how he managed to get the plane for the weekend."

"An accountant for a small firm who can afford to whisk your sister off in a private jet . . . don't you think that's a bit odd?"

Under his steady gaze, it did sound a bit odd. Still, I might not know too much about Warren, but he seemed like a good guy. Felicity was so happy. "Not at all. Daniel and Laura both seemed to know him very well. People do favors for each other all the time."

"Perhaps," he said. I got the distinct impression he was suspicious of both me and Warren. I suppose that is what he got paid to do. But I know I didn't do anything wrong and I was just as certain Warren didn't, either.

Officer Vandall stood. "I'd like you to stay here while I talk to airport security. I may have more questions."

"Is it going to take long?" I asked.

"Do you have someplace you need to be?" He raised an eyebrow as he towered over me.

"Yes, actually." I stuck my chin out. "Do I need to call my lawyer?" I lifted my phone and pretended to look through my contacts. In real life I was too poor to have an attorney. Let alone have one stored in my contacts. But he didn't need to know that.

"If you're feeling up to it, you can go," he said, his expression never changing so I had no idea if he was angry or curious as to why I wanted to call my lawyer. "I will need your address and phone number."

"Thank you." I gave him the address to my tiny apartment in Arlington Heights, and then stood to leave. Unfortunately I wasn't really ready to stand up. Maybe it was my nerves, perhaps it was all the excitement, but I had a head rush. My vision started to close up again and my legs felt rubbery. "Or maybe I'll wait a minute."

"Take your time." Officer Vandall nodded and opened the door. He stopped at the entrance. "Oh, and Ms. Pomeroy, I wouldn't leave town if I were you. We may have more questions."

"Right." I nodded and watched him walk out. He wore a

bulletproof vest under his uniform. It gave him a smooth, stiff torso. The man had a nice backside and brown hair that was the color of mahogany. Perhaps it would have been okay to spend a little more time in Officer Vandall's company.

That thought made me realize I had definitely had a bit too much excitement. Besides, my boyfriend, Bobby, was waiting for me at the Naked Truth, a hangout bar close to his apartment. It was time to get out of here.

As I stood, I noticed the two paramedics go by the office window pushing a stretcher with a large black bag on top.

It struck me as incongruous that they basically haul out the body in a big black trash bag. I waited a moment for them to take the body, put it in the ambulance, shut the doors, and leave. It felt too weird to follow the dead guy out—better to give them some space.

By the time I left the hangar, Officer Vandall was deep in conversation with Jeb Donaldson. I picked up my left-over bags and made my way to my car. An unmarked dark sedan was parked near the patrol cars, blocking my car. I sighed, put the bags in the backseat with the remaining palm, and went inside.

Officer Vandall stopped talking when he saw me. "Remember something?" he asked.

Jeb gave me a squinty-eyed look. I figured he was probably angry because I'd interrupted his involvement in the investigation.

"There's a sedan blocking my car," I said, playing with my car keys. "Can someone move it?"

"Hold on." Officer Vandall looked over his shoulder and into the now wide-open doorway to the ladies' room. I could see the crime scene tech hard at work. There were two men in suits and ties. I didn't remember seeing them come into the hangar. I imagine they showed up while Officer Vandall questioned me.

"Hey, Murphy, you're blocking the lady in."

One of the suits turned to look at us. He was about six feet tall, maybe forty, with thinning gray hair and savvy blue eyes. He had that worn look of a man who saw too much and cared too much. "Move it for me, will you?" He tossed keys toward Officer Vandall.

The officer caught them. "Sure."

I noticed Murphy studying me. Was he profiling me? I tried not to look guilty, which means I blushed to the roots of my hair and studied him back. He wore an ill-fitting black suit coat, black slacks, a white dress shirt, and a blue tie decorated with yellow Tweety Birds. He was stocky but not fat.

"Come on," Officer Vandall said. "I'll let you out. Mr. Donaldson will follow you to the gate." He turned to Jeb. "Make sure she gets out of here safe."

"Right." Jeb sent a short frown in my direction. It was really clear that he didn't like the fact that he would miss part of the investigation.

I followed both men out of the hangar. "I'm sure I'll be fine." I opened my car door. "I'm going to meet my boyfriend. He'll see I get home safe."

"I'd feel better if Mr. Donaldson followed you out," Officer Vandall insisted.

I shrugged and got into my car. A quick glance in the backseat told me that no one was hiding there. A girl had to check—I mean I've seen enough slasher movies to know you needed to be sure about these things.

The vanilla scent of the fragrant lei that hung around blue's rearview mirror mingled with the scent of palm and old car. There was something comforting in the everyday smells. Blue's seats were warmed by the sun and I let out a deep breath.

It only took a minute for Officer Vandall to move the car. I backed out and left. The palm in my backseat blocked my rear view of the hangar. I was glad to be on my way. I'm an event planner, not a crime-scene junky. Jeb dutifully followed me to the gate, where the kid who had let me in opened it and let me out.

I stepped on the gas as I pulled out onto Milwaukee Avenue. Yes, I drove away as fast as I could. It felt good. A half mile down the road, I slowed my pace enough that I wouldn't get pulled over. A ticket would be the icing on the cake for this day.

Chapter 5

I was wrong. The icing on the cake was finding Bobby and his best friend, Gage, in a booth at the back of the bar near the pool tables. Bobby had that look he got when he had had one too many drinks. I had to unclench my back teeth and smile as I approached the table. "Hi, guys, how's it going?" I buzzed a kiss on Gage's cheek and sat down beside Bobby. I kissed Bobby on the mouth, but I wasn't feeling it. I thought about the way Warren looked at Felicity. Bobby never looked at me like that.

"Where've you been?" Bobby asked as he flagged the waitress and motioned for her to bring another round of drinks.

"I was at the Executive Airport. I discovered a dead guy in the ladies' room."

"Wow," Gage said. "Are you okay?"

"Yes, thanks." I flashed him a grateful smile.

"What was a guy doing in the girls' room? Was he wearing a dress?" Bobby winked at Gage.

I rolled my eyes. "No, he was dressed like a guy. I have no idea why he died in there."

"Do you think he was murdered?" Gage asked.

"The cops acted like it," I said, and accepted the long-neck beer the waitress put in front of me. "But I didn't see any obvious evidence." I shrugged and took a swig of my beer. "I'm no crime-scene expert, but it looked like whoever killed him must have stuffed him in the stall along with a mop and bucket."

"Do you think they used that mop to clean up the evidence?"

"Gosh, I hadn't thought of that." I leaned forward toward Gage. "But it makes sense. I didn't see any obvious signs of what killed him. But he may have had a gash on the back of his head. He could have bled all over the place, although I didn't see a blood trail or anything."

"It's not like you're a bloodhound," Bobby teased. "Although I bet that hair of yours would collect scents like the folds in a bloodhound's face." He lifted a handful of strands in his fingers and let it fall. "Too bad you don't have the sense of smell a dog does. You might have actually been of some help to the cops." He finished the beer in his bottle with a giant swallow. "You called the cops, right?"

"Yes." I tried not to sigh. Bobby and I had been dating

since high school—eight years. Bobby had been cool back then, a jock on both the football and the baseball teams. Unfortunately Bobby had changed little since he was seventeen. What was cool when I was a teenager was not so cool now.

I looked at Gage. Unlike Bobby, Gage had gone to college and graduated with a business degree. He worked for a large prop house that stored scenery and such from the many local movie shoots and theater productions. I had no idea why he still hung out with Bobby. Maybe it was loyalty. Gage was like that. Once he decided on something, it stuck.

I rested my chin on my fist, elbow on the table, and studied Gage. He had short dark brown hair and must have come straight from work. He wore a pale blue dress shirt with the sleeves rolled up to his elbows. His dark blue and white striped tie was loosened. The color reflected the blue of his eyes, which were framed in thick black lashes any redhead would give her eyeteeth for.

He was the opposite of Bobby, who wore a NASCAR T-shirt with a grease stain on the shoulder and worn jeans. Gage glanced up and caught my stare. I straightened and played with the condensation on my bottle. I'm glad it was dim in the bar. No one could see my blush. Gage was taken. He was dating a cute blonde named Emma. Her family was from Lake Forest and had money.

They made a great couple. Unlike me, her hair was always perfect. She was in great shape—thin with large boobs. Her nails and makeup were always done up, and the outfits . . . needless to say, my Target skinny jeans and green sweater didn't even come close to the quality of her cashmere sweaters and designer slacks.

Not that I wanted to have to worry about always looking put together. I had enough things on my mind. But Gage had good taste in women. Not only was Emma well groomed but she was educated and worked downtown at a fancy marketing firm.

"So what the heck were you doing at the Executive Airport anyway? You get a job out there cleaning toilets?" Bobby snorted as if what he'd said was funny.

I winced. "Felicity got engaged to Warren tonight. He asked me to set up the event for him, remember?"

"No," Bobby said as the waitress put a fresh beer in front of him. Gage waved off another round. I clung to my nearly full bottle as a clear sign I wasn't buying more. Beer at a bar cost twice what a homemade margarita did. Warren's check in my pocket could be put to better use than buying Bobby drinks. "I can't keep up with what you're doing . . . not working, though. Find a job yet?"

"No." I rolled my eyes at Bobby's inference that I was some kind of deadbeat. Gage gave me a sympathetic look over his half-empty bottle of beer. "Anyway, Warren does accounting work for this company that has a private jet. They let him rent it," I told Gage since he seemed more interested than Bobby. "I decorated the inside with mementoes of their dating life. Felicity had no idea what was coming until he got down on one knee." I pressed my hand to my chest. "It was so romantic. We all clapped when she said yes and then they flew off to a romantic destination."

"They flew off to a romantic destination," Bobby mocked and then took a swig of his beer. "Who does that?"

"Warren, I suppose," I answered. It was times like this when I wondered why we were still together. Complacency, I guessed. Maybe we were both too lazy to move on. I mean, after eight years, I felt as if I'd invested a lot of time in Bobby. I kept waiting for the confident, competent Bobby from high school to come back. I think for Bobby, I was just the girl who was here. He didn't have to do anything—not even listen to me tell him where I was going.

I had tried for years to get him to go out into the world. I'd dragged him to event after event that I had planned and worried over, trying to amuse him. But he preferred to either be here at the bar playing pool and getting drunk or home in front of the TV drinking beer. Either way I was an afterthought. Like an appendage, I was simply there.

The realization hit me like a bolt out of the blue. I could live alone and still not be heard, but then there might be space for someone else in my life. I mean, there had to be more guys like Gage out there, didn't there?

"What are you pouting about?" Bobby scowled at me.

"I'm not pouting." I frowned at him. "I was just thinking how I want something like that."

"To be flown away for a weekend?" Gage asked.

"No," I sighed. "To have someone who cares enough to make things special for me."

It was then that I looked at Bobby. Really looked at him. I think that was the truth of it—I wanted him to care enough to make something special for me. Deep in my heart of hearts, I knew he never would.

Bobby got a little surly when he saw me looking through him. "Is that what's been bugging you lately?" he asked, missing the point entirely. "You want me to propose?"

"Oh, gosh no." I shook my head. It was so strange; I'd been waiting for years for Bobby to propose, but after seeing Warren look at Felicity, I couldn't do it. I couldn't imagine marrying a man who looked at me as a pain in the bum. That was the look Bobby gave me right then.

"Right." Bobby narrowed his eyes. "You've been hinting at it for years, and now your sister is engaged. You'll really start hounding me."

"No, really," I protested. "I don't want you to propose."

He sneered at me. "Good because you're nuts if you think I'm going to get down on one knee in this place." He waved his beer bottle at the sticky, filthy, peanut-shell-encrusted floor.

"I don't want you to get down on one knee," I said as clearly as I could. For such a long time I had hoped that he would propose. That he would think to ask my sister or my friends what I would want—a sunset picnic by a lake. He never did ask, and now I could see he never would.

"Good." He took a swig of his drink. "So I suppose you want to then."

"Want to what?" I could hear the horror in my voice.

"Get married," he said with a snarl.

Looking at the disdain rolling off him, I realized I had invested far too much of my time in a man who didn't love me.

"No," I said as firmly as I could. "I want to break up." I got up and walked out. There was a rush of relief. I realized suddenly that I would be okay on my own. Far better than to be stuck with a man who spent all his free hours in a dingy bar, playing pool and listening to out-of-date tunes on the jukebox.

After all, I'd discovered a dead body. I'd called the cops. After that there wasn't much that could faze me—certainly not the sound of Bob Seger singing "Against the Wind." How old was that song anyway? The music was as old as the bar.

The night air was cool as I shoved the door open. The scent was crisp and clean and free of stale beer and musty peanuts. I really was going to be okay. I had not only discovered a body, but I'd put together a romantic proposal personalized for Felicity.

Maybe Warren was right. Maybe I could start my own business. He'd even given me enough seed money to live on for six months. I would be foolish not to try.

First thing tomorrow I would make up business cards. When Felicity and Warren got back, I would ask them both to hand them out to clients or friends. Surely if there was one considerate, caring man like Warren, there had to be two.

At least that was what I would stake my life on for the next six months.

My heart felt light. I took another deep breath of fresh air. For the first time in a long time, I felt as if I was on the right path. Maybe, just maybe, I could make something out of the ruins of my life.

Chapter 6

Two days later I was at my parents' home helping Mom with Sunday dinner.

"What's with the china?" my dad, Frank Pomeroy, asked as he passed through the dining room of the brick bungalow my parents had lived in my entire life.

"We're celebrating," my mom, Abigail, said without a blink. She carefully folded her best linen napkins into tiny pockets for the silverware.

"What?" Dad asked. "Did I forget an anniversary?"

"Felicity and Warren are flying home this afternoon," I said as I put out the silverware.

"I made my famous pot roast," Mom stated. "I thought you could smell it."

"I can." Dad shoved his big workman's hands in his pockets. Dad was tall, around six feet three inches. He used to be six feet four, but he had started to shrink with age. He didn't look bad for a man in his late fifties. He still had a full head of hair, although it had gone from red to white pretty early. His blue eyes sparkled with intelligence. Today he wore a light blue denim work shirt and dark blue jeans. My whole life Dad had been a plumber. He was proud of his profession and belonged to the local plumbers' union. His favorite television show was *Ghost Hunters* because the two main guys were also plumbers.

"I figured there was a sale on roast or something," he said.

"You did not," I teased. "I saw you run out of the house the minute you realized it was pot roast."

"What is she talking about, Frank?" Mom straightened and studied my dad.

He shrugged. "Like I said, I thought it was an anniversary or something."

"Oh, he bought you a present," I said then clamped my hand over my mouth when my father glared at me.

"Frank, you didn't." Mom's green eyes twinkled.

"He did," I said and then bit my lip as my dad narrowed his gaze at me.

Mom came around the table. "You bought me a present?"

"It can wait." Dad blushed. Like me, he could never hide a blush. His ears turned bright pink whenever he was embarrassed or put on the spot. Even though his hair was completely white, he still had the skin of a redhead. It showed emotions like the colors of an octopus.

"It most certainly cannot." Mom held out her hand. "Give it to me . . . please."

"Fine." Dad pulled a long box out of his pocket. "Think of it as a mother-of-the-bride gift."

Mom opened the box and took out a silver charm bracelet. There were three starter beads on it. One was a piano. Mom was a part-time piano teacher and spent her Saturdays teaching students at one of two pianos in the music room. The music room was actually our basement, which Dad had finished on his own. He'd put in a drop ceiling and painted the cinder block walls. A Berber carpet and two upright pianos had given Mom the space she needed to teach her lessons without impinging on his football games.

The second bead was a silver bride, and the third charm was . . . "Is that a cuckoo bird?" I had to ask because I hoped for something better to represent me.

"What a cute cuckoo bird it is, too." Mom brushed a kiss on Dad's lips. "You'll get your reward later, even if it isn't an anniversary."

Dad grinned.

Mom might be described as curvy, but Dad didn't seem to mind the extra bits of her. She was the shortest in the family at five feet two inches tall. She wore a size fourteen and tended to be a progressive dresser. Today she had on a pair of dark slacks and a light green sweater set that played up the color in her eyes. She kept her hair dyed a dark brown and cut short so that it curled like a pixie around her face.

"Pepper, help me with this clasp, will you, honey?" She held out her wrist and I clasped the charm bracelet. "What do you think?"

"It's lovely," I said. "But I'm still not certain what the cuckoo bird represents."

"Oh, probably the passing of time, dear." Mom went back to folding napkins as if I wouldn't know she was lying. "Put the crystal champagne glasses out," she said. "It's not every day we get to have champagne."

Mom had pink-toned Irish crystal champagne glasses that I'd only seen her use a handful of times. The last time was on my parents' thirtieth wedding anniversary.

I pulled the glasses out of the china cabinet and wiped them off with a soft cloth before I placed them on the table.

"There, isn't the table lovely?" Mom asked, admiring our handiwork.

"I do know how to set a table," I said and put my hands on my hips. "It was part of event planning 101."

"I know, dear." Mom patted my arm as she moved to the kitchen. "It's nice to see you use your degree."

"I use my degree a lot." I followed her into the kitchen.

She grabbed kitchen mitts decorated with red and green roosters and opened the oven to check the roast.

The rich scent of roasted meat and onion filled the air. "I'm sure you do. Now if only you found a way to get paid for it."

I sat down at the small kitchen table. It was mid-century modern with a red Formica top with chrome trim and legs. The chairs were silver pipe with red vinyl cushions. I think the set had been my grandma's and she had given it to my parents when they first got married. I could admire the style in the piece. It fit perfectly in mom's tiny kitchen, tucked under the window.

The rest of the kitchen was straight out of the sixties with tall maple cabinets and white Formica countertops trimmed in stainless steel. The sink was deep and had been installed by the previous owner. To give you an idea of the age of the décor, my parents had bought the house in 1980. They loved vintage and had used that as an excuse not to update anything in the house.

The floors were wood from when the house was built in the 1920s. The walls were plaster and the doorways were arched. The house was a basic bungalow. It had a porch that ran the width of the front of the house. The front door opened into the living room. To the right was the guest bedroom. It had been my room growing up.

Straight back from the living room and separated by a wide archway was the dining room. Behind that was the kitchen, which opened to the stairs to the basement and a tiny back porch, where Mom's students would take off their shoes before they entered.

To the right of the kitchen was a small hall that led

straight into the only bathroom. To the left of the bath was my parents' room. To the right of the bath was Felicity's old room. My sister had her own apartment as well, and my parents now used her room for storage. My mother had considered making her room the new music room, but Dad refused to pull those pianos upstairs. So instead she used it as a place to keep her sewing machines and Dad's desk, where he had his computer and did his accounts.

I snatched a carrot slice off the veggie tray Mom had put on the kitchen table. "I can't wait to see the video of their engagement." I tapped my fingertips on the DVD that sat on the table. "Cesar assured me it was romantic. Then you can see what all went into planning the event."

"There had better not be any sign of that poor dead fellow in the video." Mom closed the open door. "That would be terrible, just terrible for your sister."

"There isn't," I said. "I checked. Besides Cesar gave a copy of the video to Detective Murphy. I'm certain the detective on the case would not have let us keep a copy if there was any evidence on it."

"What an awful thing, finding a dead man in the ladies' room." My mom tsked her tongue and pulled out a package of brown-and-serve rolls and placed them in a pan. "Did you ever find out who he was?"

"There was no identification on him," I said. "Last I heard, they were going to check missing persons and see if anyone fit his description."

"Will they tell you when they find out?"

"I don't suppose they will." I shrugged and grabbed another carrot. "There would be no reason to tell me."

"But aren't you a witness or something?" Mom asked.

"I found the body, but I didn't see anyone or anything unusual." I sat back and studied my mom. She had her own small business. Maybe she would appreciate my idea. I'd been thinking about my business plan all weekend. But it would have to pass my parents' sniff test before I could even consider it. "So, Mom, Warren said I should go into business for myself."

"Really? What would you do?" Mom wiped her hands on a dish towel.

"I'm thinking of event planning in a niche market," I said and rested my head against the orange-and-yellow-floral-wallpaper-covered wall. She looked at me blankly. "I could do proposal events. Warren said I did a great job helping him plan Felicity's proposal."

"I don't understand how you can make a living at that," Mom said carefully. "A gentleman in love buys a ring, takes his lady to a nice restaurant and gets down on one knee. What's to plan? Speaking of gentlemen, where's Bobby? It's not like him not to come to a family dinner— especially when there's free food."

"We broke up." I reached for a piece of celery.

"You broke up?" Mom scrunched her brows. "Why? When? Are you okay?"

"What happened?" Dad asked as he strolled back into the kitchen and pinched a cookie off the dessert tray Mom had on the counter.

"Pepper and Bobby broke up." Mom slapped Dad's hand when he reached for a second cookie. "Dinner's almost ready."

Dad pretended nothing happened and pulled a glass out of the cupboard and filled it with water from the fridge. "It's about time," he said. "That guy was a deadbeat."

"I thought you liked Bobby," I said. The celery suddenly tasted like cardboard.

"Oh, honey, that was high school. We thought you'd lose interest in him when you went away to college."

"Why else would we let you go off to DePauw when there are a number of good schools right here in Chicago?" Dad said.

"But I thought . . ." I frowned and shook my head. "Never mind."

"At least you weren't living with him," Dad said. He gave me the evil eye. "You weren't, were you?"

"No." I glared back at him. "Bobby likes his own space."

"Well, I'm glad you didn't marry him." Mom hung the towel on the oven door.

"Did he break up with you?" Dad asked. "Because if he did, I may have to go teach him a lesson."

"No, Dad." I tried hard not to roll my eyes. "I broke up with him."

"That's my smart girl." He planted a kiss on my forehead as he headed toward the dining room.

The front door opened, Felicity and Warren stepped inside, and all talk of me and my love life ended. Mom rushed to greet my sister with a hug and a kiss and squeals. I hugged my waist and smiled at the joy on their faces. Dad shook hands with Warren and patted him on the back.

"Welcome to the family, son." Dad had always wanted a boy. Living in a houseful of women, he often felt outnumbered.

I stepped in and gave my sister a kiss and a hug. Then I hugged Warren. Mom took their coats, putting them on the bed in the front bedroom, and went to the kitchen to serve appetizers.

Mom and Dad's living room was classic in design with pale green walls and darker green carpeting. One wall of windows was covered with green and cream patterned drapery. The overstuffed couch sat in front of it. Across from the couch were two stuffed chairs with a tiny table between them. The couch was dark green with bright poppy red pillows.

Mom had a neutral area rug on top of the carpet to define the space. I would call her decorating taste seventies chic. What really made it were the eagle lamps in a bronze tone.

"How was your trip?" Dad asked as Felicity and Warren sat down on the couch. "Where'd you go?" Dad took his favorite chair across from them.

"Oh, it was so wonderful," Felicity said, her eyes sparkling. "Warren took me to New York City. We stayed in a hotel downtown, went to a Broadway show, and had dinner at this French bistro named Beloit. The next morning we went ring shopping." Felicity held out her hand to show off a large marquise-cut diamond.

"Oh, my word." My mother went breathless at the sight. She handed me the platter she'd brought in from the kitchen and grabbed my sister's hand. "Pepper, look at this."

"Wow," I said. "It's lovely."

"That had to set you back." Dad frowned. "You should have saved your money for a down payment on a house."

"Actually, there are a couple of things we need to tell you," Warren said.

"What kind of things?" Dad narrowed his eyes.

I had a funny feeling something was up. Seriously, the rock on my sister's finger had to have cost in the tens of thousands of dollars. How could Warren afford it on an accountant's salary?

My thoughts went to the cost of the private jet and the trip. This was Chicago. There was money around and not all of it good. Exactly who did Warren work for?

Chapter 7

"Bad things?" Mom asked as she took the tray from me and passed around her famous canapés. I found myself standing in concern as my sister stared lovingly at her fiancé.

"There's good news and bad news," Felicity said, her gaze never leaving Warren's face.

"Did you rob a bank or something?" My father joked then his face grew solemn. "Better not have."

Warren's grin widened. "No, no, nothing like that."

"Good." Dad nodded and crossed his arms over his chest.

"Does it have to do with the dead man at the airport?" I blurted out.

I noticed a tick in Warren's jaw at my question.

"Pepper!" Felicity scolded.

"It does, doesn't it?" I went in for the kill. I could always tell when my sister was hiding something, and today's something had to be a doozy.

"Actually, that's the bad news." Warren patted Felicity's hand. "We're late because the police wanted to question us both the minute we got back."

"Both of yooze?" Dad's expression grew concerned. His eyebrows veed and his mouth tightened. "Felicity, tell me you did not let them question you without a lawyer present."

"Don't worry," Warren said. "I called my lawyers."

"You called your lawyers? What does an accountant need with lawyers? Or are they your boss's lawyers?" I found myself planting my feet wide and putting my fisted hands on my hips. I was ready to punch this guy. How could Felicity say yes to a man who acted so out of character?

"Warren's really rich," Felicity blurted out.

"What?" Mom and I asked at the same time.

How could Warren be rich? He didn't wear fancy clothes. He wore suits from chain department stores. He drove a Volvo, for crying out loud.

"How can he be rich?" I asked. How well did Felicity know Warren anyway?

"I have a trust fund," Warren said. "I'm worth half a billion dollars. My grandfather was an oilman in Texas. My father took his trust money and made a killing in stocks."

"Why did we not know this?" Mom asked. "Felicity? Did you know and not tell us?"

It hit me suddenly that the reason for his large check was because he could afford to pay me. It all seemed so odd. We were comfortably middle class. Our family didn't know the first thing about trust funds or lawyers or private jets, for that matter.

"I only found out this weekend," Felicity said. "The jet is Warren's private business jet. Daniel and Laura work for Warren."

"You own the jet?" I couldn't believe it. Who owns a jet?

"I don't like to talk about my money," Warren said. "I've had some really bad experiences dating women who only saw dollar signs when they looked at me. I wanted a woman who loved me for me, not for my fortune." He turned to Felicity. "So when I met Felicity, I told her the truth. I am an accountant—who happens to also have millions in trust."

"You lied to her?" Dad growled.

"No, sir," Warren said. "I simply left off the part about my trust fund."

"Warren studied accounting so that he could best manage his money," Felicity said. "He runs a charity foundation. He told me about it, but I thought he volunteered there. I had no idea he actually ran it."

"You run a charity foundation?" Mom asked and fanned herself. "Oh, my."

"The plane is simply one of a number of diverse investments I own. I bought it to help the foundation. I promise you, sir. I will take good care of your daughter. I set out to find someone who loves me for me. I found her."

"I think it's time for the champagne," Dad said. "I hope you don't mind that it's the cheaper stuff."

"Warren doesn't mind." Felicity patted his knee. "Don't treat him like he's any different than us. He's an accountant who just happens to own a private jet and a couple of homes in Europe."

Oh, man, I thought. How could Warren keep a secret as big as this from Felicity?

"It's why the police wanted to question us," Warren said. I watched as he squeezed my sister's hand. "I'm connected to the airport and the dead man."

"You are? How?" I asked and had to restrain myself from yanking my sister away from the suspicious man beside her. "As far as I know, they haven't released the man's identity yet."

"His name was Randy Stromer," Warren said. "He worked as a janitor at the airport. Since I own a forty-nine percent share of the airport and rent out hangar four, the police had to question me. It happened on my property."

"Why did they question Felicity?" I asked.

"They were simply covering all their bases. I explained to them that Felicity didn't know about my ownership in the airport or about who worked there. They were fine with my answer."

"Felicity, is this true?" Mom asked. I noted how she wrung her hands. It was a nervous tick she had whenever one of her babies was threatened.

"Yes, of course, Mama." Felicity kissed Mom on the cheek. "I'm fine, really. Warren's lawyers did a great job. The police will have to get a warrant and offer just cause to interview us again."

"If it didn't mean anything, why was it bad news?" Mom asked.

"When we went to leave, the detective in charge . . . what was his name?"

"Murphy," I answered my sister. Everyone looked at me funny. "What? He was the guy at the crime scene."

"You found the body, right?" Warren asked me.

"Yes." I nodded.

"Then you know there is no way Felicity or I was involved. Did you tell the police that?"

"Of course I did," I answered and crossed my arms in front of me.

"I'm going to get the champagne." Mom went back into the kitchen.

"Are you going to make her sign one of those pre-nups?" Dad asked while Mom was in the kitchen. "Because we don't believe in those things."

"No, we talked it over." Warren and Felicity looked at each other with devotion. "Felicity will be my wife. I love her and will support her my entire life no matter what happens."

"Good!" Dad slapped Warren on the back. "Again, welcome to the family."

"Champagne!" Mom came in with a tray loaded down with her crystal flutes.

I took my glass after Felicity and Warren. Mom handed Dad his glass and, tucking the tray under her arm, raised hers. "To the happy couple."

"Hear, hear!"

"Cheers!"

I watched as my family saluted the happy couple. When I took a small sip of my champagne, I noted the starry-eyed look on Felicity's face and couldn't help wondering. If Warren had kept something as big as a multimillion-dollar trust fund from my sister, what else was he keeping from her?

Chapter 8

"Are you okay with all this?" I asked as I dried the dishes.

Felicity paused from her washing and sent me this sweet dopey smile. "I simply can't believe it. I mean, the proposal was out of this world. It was everything I'd ever dreamed it would be." She plunged her pink-gloved hands back into the sudsy water and pulled out a plate. "Warren tells me you helped him stage the whole event."

"I did," I said. "But I had no idea he had a trust fund or that the airplane belonged to him. He lied to me and told me he was renting it for a good rate because he did some work for the company."

"He lied because he wanted to tell me first and he couldn't tell me until we were engaged." She wiped the plate with a sponge, rinsed it, and put it in the drainer.

"I'm glad he didn't tell you. I'm glad he told me first. I should have been told first, don't you think?"

"I think he should have been honest with you from the start." I picked up the plate and wiped it with a dish towel. I could hear Mom and Dad and Warren laughing and talking in the front room.

"He had good reasons not to tell me." Felicity shrugged. "I don't think I would have even dated him had I known." She paused and leaned against the counter, dampening the towel she had pinned around her waist. "The whole weekend was so incredible. He told me right after we took off. The flight was smooth and everything was perfect. He took my hand and confessed everything. When we landed in New York, there was a stretch limo waiting to pick us up." She shook her head. "We stayed in this incredible hotel and ordered room service. He took me for a carriage ride around Central Park. The next day we toured museums and that night he took me to see a Broadway musical. Then we went to dinner at a swanky restaurant that had floor-to-ceiling windows. Pepper, you could look out over the skyline." She sighed. "It was like being on top of the world."

I cringed inwardly at her joy. I hoped that my suspicions were groundless. For Felicity's sake . . . she deserved the best in a relationship. So did I, for that matter.

"Felicity, we need to plan your engagement party," Mom said as she entered the room. "You could have Pepper plan the event for you. She's thinking of opening her own event-planning business."

"You are?" Felicity asked me as she put the last dish in the drainer and removed her pink rubber gloves.

"It was Warren's idea," I said. "Of course, start-up money is always an issue, my being out of work and all."

"I don't see why you can't move back home," my father said from the kitchen doorway. "It's silly for you to keep that tiny apartment when you are unemployed. You should come home until you get back on your feet. Right, dear?"

"Yes, of course," my mother said. "I could even divide the music room and you could have your own office for your event planning."

I swallowed my horror at their invitation. It'd taken me so long to get out on my own. The last thing I wanted was to live with my parents when I was thirty. "Gee, thanks, Dad, thanks, Mom, but my apartment isn't that expensive and it's near the mall. So I'll have access to more ideas and materials."

"What's going on?" Warren stood behind Dad.

"Pepper's going to open her own event-planning business," Felicity said and took the towel off her waist. "Isn't that great?"

"Fantastic," Warren said. His blue eyes twinkled.

"Thanks, I had good inspiration," I said.

"Speaking of inspiration, let's talk about your engagement party," Mom said. We all adjourned to the living room.

"We are going to wait on the engagement party," Felicity said, her gaze never leaving Warren. He put his arm around her waist and nodded.

"Why would you do that?" Mom asked as we all sat.

"It's only until after the investigation," Warren said.

Felicity put her hand on his knee. "We felt it was in poor taste to party while they investigate that poor man's murder."

"It's simply better to wait until after the police have made an arrest," Warren added. "Don't you agree?"

"Makes sense," Dad said

"Fine." Mom leaned forward and clasped her hands. "How long do you think they will be investigating?"

"I have no idea." Felicity frowned as if she hadn't quite thought that part through.

It struck me that murder investigations could take years. My next thought was worse. What if after five or more years, they determined Warren had something to do with the murder? Felicity would already be married and possibly even have children.

Something had to be done about that.

"You don't want to wait too long to announce your engagement, do you?" Mom had that hopeful look in her eyes.

Felicity looked at Warren. "No, not really."

"If I had it my way, I would have screamed it from the rooftops on Friday." Warren raised their joined hands and kissed her knuckles. "But seriously, the man had a family. How can we put on an appropriate party when he is lying in the morgue?"

"I suppose that's true." Mom sat back and did not hide her disappointment. "I'll have to ask my friend Doris what the proper waiting period is for something like this."

"Yes, do. Doris knows more than Miss Manners sometimes." Felicity's gaze brightened. "In the meantime, we could plan the party, couldn't we?"

"I don't see why not," Warren said. "Pepper, what do you think? Would you consider planning the event?"

"Yes, Pepper, please?"

"Okay," I agreed. After all, Warren had given me the idea to start my own business. The least I could do was plan my sister's engagement party. In fact, that might make a great package deal—proposal and engagement. After all, I would know what the bride-to-be wanted, wouldn't I?

"That's settled, then." Mom stood. "Come on, girls, let's coordinate our calendars. Oh, Felicity, I know the perfect woman to sing at your wedding . . . and Mrs. Shelton can play the organ . . ."

I followed them into the kitchen. My thoughts were less on the planning and more on how I would figure out if Warren was guilty or not before this engagement got too far.

Chapter 9

"What are you doing here?" Officer Vandall asked.

"I wondered if you needed anything further from me for your investigation," I said. I had dressed like a professional so that the police would take me seriously. A quick glance around told me that they didn't deal with professionally dressed people too often. Besides, I didn't want to come off as a kook.

I tugged my navy skirt down to ensure it hit at my knee. The fabric had a way of hiking up when I walked. Mom used to tell me all the time to slow down and walk like a lady so that wouldn't happen. Some things a girl never learns.

Officer Vandall tilted his head. "Did you remember something else?"

I recognized that as a gatekeeper question. I was prepared to lie. "I have information about Warren Evans." That statement was true, and my skin stayed blushless as he eyed me.

He glanced at me and his mouth pursed. "Fine. I'll see if Detective Murphy has time to talk to you now."

"Thank you."

Officer Vandall went through the door that I assumed led to the officers' cubicles. I was left to cool my heels in the waiting area out front. I took a moment to check that the patterned blouse I wore was appropriately buttoned. The thin belt at my waist had not slid to the left.

My hair, well, I had learned long ago that it had a mind of its own. We had come to a deal. I didn't expect it to do anything fashionable and it didn't stick out . . . too much.

"Ms. Pomeroy?" I glanced up to see the hound dog face of Detective Murphy. He wasn't unattractive. He had that older Humphrey Bogart kind of look. It made you think he put on a fedora when he walked out the door. Today his broad shoulders were encased in a white shirt. A red and blue striped tie was pulled loose at his neck. Black dress slacks and standard-issue black dress shoes finished the look. Even if I hadn't known he was a police detective, I would have imagined that he was.

"Yes, hello again." I held out my hand.

He shook it. "Detective Murphy. Officer Vandall told me you have information on the airport murder?"

"I was the one who called 911," I said.

"Yes, I know." He opened the door wide. "Why don't

you come back and we'll chat. Can I get you some coffee? It's cop coffee, but it'll do in a pinch."

"I'm fine, thank you." I followed him down a hall that was made by the edge of cubicles and a wall that held windows and doors. From what I could tell, the doors led to small rooms. I had watched enough *48 Hours* to know they were most likely interview rooms.

His office was in the room at the end of the hall. The room was about twelve feet by twelve feet and held four desks, a bank of file cabinets, and two printers. It smelled of stale coffee and aftershave.

"Have a seat." He waved me toward a chair next to a desk with his name plaque. I noticed that he had the desk farthest from the door and his back was to a wall.

I sat in the green plastic chair, my purse on my lap and my hands gripping the handle. I took a deep breath and blew it out slowly. It was kind of scary in the police station. Odd to think I was more frightened in here than I was when I found the body. Maybe because the man was dead. While Detective Murphy looked as if he could read my every thought.

I steeled myself. "Do you know his name? The dead guy . . . That night all Officer Vandall would tell me is that he didn't have any identification on him."

"His name was Randy Stromer. Jeb Donaldson identified him."

I shook my head. "I don't know a Randy Stromer. I've never heard Warren speak of him." Okay, so that was a white lie. It was Warren who had told me his name.

"He was a janitor at the airport. It's how he got through security. We figured he was an employee as Donaldson didn't have a record of any other nonpassengers besides you and your video man."

"Do you have a motive? I mean, why would anyone want to kill a janitor?"

"That's the question, isn't it?" Murphy sat back. "Did you have information for me, Ms. Pomeroy, or did you have another motive for coming by?"

I blinked. "My sister is engaged to Warren Evans."

"I think that's in the report." His gaze was flat.

"She is my baby sister and I need to know if marrying Warren Evans is right for my sister or not." I clutched my purse. "Felicity said you had a lot of questions for them and that Warren called in his lawyer."

"I do have a lot of questions," Detective Murphy said.

"Is my sister in trouble?"

"You tell me, because she wouldn't."

I frowned. "That doesn't sound like Felicity. Besides, I know she wasn't at the airport until after five. I was there when she got there and I'd already . . ."

"You already what?" He leaned forward.

"Decorated the plane," I said. "Before she got there. I decorated the plane and Cesar went up and hid himself."

"Are you withholding evidence? Because that is a crime." He gave me the serious look of a parent who already knew their child was guilty.

I could feel the heat of a blush race up my neck. "Is it hot in here?" I asked and fanned myself.

"You're avoiding the question. Are you withholding evidence?"

"No," I said as sincerely as possible. "No. I need to know what you know about Warren."

"I can't reveal anything about the investigation." He leaned back. "You know that."

"You can tell me how seriously you are looking at Warren Evans."

"You suspect something, don't you?" he asked.

"Did you know he is wealthy?"

"Yes, he owns forty-nine percent of the private airline at the Executive Airport. The company owns three private jets and leases them along with the mechanics and pilots."

"See, he's been seeing Felicity for over a year and lied to her the entire time. He told her he was an accountant and that he worked for the airport."

"Both of those things are technically true," Detective Murphy said.

I crossed my arms. "Is he a suspect or not?"

"I can't tell you."

I stood. "Then I'm sorry for taking up your time."

"Ms. Pomeroy . . ." He stopped me. "Take my card. You look like a determined person. If you come across anything you think I might need to know, call me."

I took his card. "I wish I could ask the same of you."

"Have a good day."

"Right." As I walked out, I passed Officer Vandall talking to another officer I recognized from the crime scene.

"Evans is our number one suspect," he said to the other

officer. Then I heard the word *blackmail* before they grew quiet.

"Have a nice day, gentlemen." I pushed my way through the doors to the waiting area and my car. Officer Vandall knew I was in with Detective Murphy. I figured I was meant to overhear what he said.

Why would Warren kill a janitor? How did blackmail fit in? I had thirty days to find out.

Chapter 10

"Hey, Miss Pomeroy, what are you doing here?" The kid who sat in the guard shack at the entrance to the airport looked a little less bored today.

"Hi, Jimmy, I brought you cupcakes." I lifted the lid on a tin holding a wide variety of cakes. "Can I come in?"

"Wow, are those chocolate?" His blue eyes grew wide.

"Yes, and fudge and mocha and vanilla swirl and chocolate chip. I'm trying to figure out what to serve at my sister's engagement party. I need a second opinion and remembered that you were here. You look like a guy who likes a good cupcake."

"I do like a good cupcake." Jimmy was as skinny as

any twenty-something could be. His blond hair flopped forward in his eyes. His tan security uniform appeared to be pressed this time. He hit the button that raised the arm of the gate and I drove into the parking spot beside the guard shack. I looked at the cupcakes. Bribery seemed to be my best idea yet. I hoped I could get some information out of Jimmy. Anything would be more than Detective Murphy gave me.

Jimmy opened the door to the tiny guard shack and let me inside. There was room for two people, two stools that were bar height, and a counter that held a coffeepot, some mugs, and a microwave.

I handed him the platter of cupcakes and took a seat on the stool away from the window. Should Jeb decide to come by, I didn't want him to see me right off. "Wow, you have electricity in here?" I asked and pointed to the appliance.

Jimmy sat down on his stool and put the cupcakes in his lap. "Yeah, gets cold in the winter, so Jeb thought coffee would be good. Trouble with that is you have to . . . well, you know . . . go a lot when you drink."

"I see." I looked around. There definitely was not another room in the shack. "How do you take care of that?"

He picked up a double-chocolate cupcake and peeled off the paper holder. "Hangar number one." He bit into the cake and closed his eyes in joy.

"Who watches the gate while you . . . you know . . . go?"

"I call Jeb. Sometimes he comes out. Sometimes he watches the cameras." Jimmy devoured the cupcake in a second bite and picked up another. This one was chocolate chip with fudge icing.

"You have cameras?"

"Sure, everyone does. It's standard security." He took two more quick bites and finished off the second cupcake.

"Do the police know?"

"Yeah." He picked up an orange Dreamsicle cupcake. This one was orange cake with white cream filling and orange butter cream frosting on top. "Cops took all the tapes. Pissed Jeb off because he had to go buy all new ones. We generally use the same ones and tape over them."

Tilting my head thoughtfully, I watched as he ate the orange cake in one bite. "You still use actual tapes? I would think you would have that all digitized."

"Naw, it's an old system. Jeb says it's good enough for our low rate of crime. Might digitize now, though. It's hard to replace tapes. Not too many people selling them anymore."

"Well, that's certainly true." My mom had been complaining that all her movies on VCR tapes would have to be bought again as DVDs and that at the rate technology was changing she didn't want to invest in DVDs only to have to replace them all again in five years with whatever was new. "How many tapes were there?"

Jimmy swallowed his mouthful of cupcake.

I handed him a napkin from the stack on the counter near the coffeepot. "You have orange stuff on your cheek."

"Thanks." He wiped at it, effectively smearing it across his face. "Don't know for sure how many tapes. We have cameras set up every hundred yards around the perimeter of the airport. Then there are cameras that are pointed at the hangar doors."

"That's a lot of footage."

He downed two more cupcakes. The kid was skinny as a rail. I had no idea where he was putting it all. If I so much as smelled a cupcake, I gained five pounds on each thigh and not in a good curvy way.

"Not really." He shrugged. "Only half the cameras work."

"Only half? Won't someone unauthorized get in?"

"Naw, see, Jeb had them set to randomly turn on and off. There's no way to tell which cameras are recording and which aren't. He said it was ingenious and it saves the company a couple grand a year."

"Interesting . . . Who knows about the cameras? Being random, I mean?"

Jimmy shrugged and finished off the cakes on the platter. "I do and Jeb . . . I suppose the rest of the crew does."

"Does management? I mean, someone like Warren Evans, would he know?"

"Sure, he signed off on the thing when Jeb proposed it."

That was not a good sign. "Do the cops know about that?"

"Don't know." Jimmy twisted and reached behind him. There was a mini fridge under the cabinet. He pulled out a bottle of water and offered me one.

"Thanks." I twisted off the cap and sipped. Jimmy guzzled his own bottle. "Surely Jeb told the investigators."

Jimmy frowned. "Can't see why he would. The tapes cover random spots. There really is no way to tell what was turned on and what wasn't."

"Aren't they time stamped?"

"Oh, huh, maybe . . . sure. I suppose they could tell then."

I twirled my bottle of water between my fingers. "I was questioned for a long time about what I saw. It was really tough to remember. Did the police question you, too?"

"Yeah." Jimmy nodded. "They asked all kinds of questions. I told them what I know. Jeb said that was the right thing to do."

"Was it difficult?"

"Naw, I have a good memory."

"I heard it was a janitor that was killed."

"Yeah, poor Stromer. The guy had his troubles, but he didn't need to be killed over it."

"Right?" I agreed. "I mean, who doesn't have troubles these days."

"I know, especially when you have a gambling problem." Jimmy looked both ways as if someone else might overhear and leaned in toward me. "I hear he was in deep with the casinos. He even sold his house."

"Ouch." I winced.

Jimmy's mouth curled and he shrugged. "Didn't stop him. He thought he could win it all back, but that didn't work. Them casinos sucker you in."

"What did he do once his house was gone?"

Jimmy looked around again. "I hear he had something over Mr. Evans."

"You mean, he tried to blackmail Warren Evans?"

"No, I mean, he told him he knew his secret, and if Mr. Evans wanted him to keep his mouth shut, he'd have to pay."

"I see." I sat back. Things were not looking good for Warren or Felicity. "Did you tell the cops this?"

"Naw, they didn't ask."

"Did anyone else know what Stromer did?"

"Sure, he bragged to everyone that he had Mr. Evans over a barrel. The guy was sure to give him a couple grand. Strom was going to win back his house and enough money to buy Mr. Evans out."

"Huh, so anyone could have told the cops about Stromer bragging he'd get money from Mr. Evans."

"Sure, I guess so." Jimmy checked out the window. "Someone's coming. You have any more cupcakes?"

"No, that was it . . . only a dozen."

"Too bad . . . you should go before Jeb sees you."

"Right." I got up and picked up the platter. "Just one thing."

"What's that?"

"Which cupcake did you like best—for my sister's engagement party . . ."

"Oh." He drew his eyebrows together. Then his expression brightened. "The chocolate ones!" He nodded and raised a finger. "Definitely chocolate, although the orange were good . . . No, chocolate. It's an engagement party and all. I think chocolate equals love or some such thing."

"Thanks." I stepped out of the shack. Okay, so there were several chocolate ones—red velvet, chocolate chip, dark chocolate. Sigh. I mentally shrugged. I didn't really want his opinion anyway. I got in my car and he opened the gate for me to drive out.

I dialed Warren.

"Hey, Pepper, how's the engagement party planning going?" he asked as he answered my call.

"Hi, Warren, things are going fine. I've got a line on a beautiful venue downtown. We never did talk budget," I said. "It's kind of important."

"Sure, sure, you know how I feel. Spare no expense. If Felicity wants it, make it happen."

"Right." I tried not to roll my eyes. "Listen, I heard that the dead janitor talked about you a lot. Did you know him well?"

"Sure." Warren sounded distracted. "I knew him. Randy Stroiner was a hard-core gambler. It was tough to see him throw away his money."

"I heard that he was blackmailing you." I let that sentence float out on the air a bit. I would have loved to ask him to his face. People gave away things in their expression, but there wasn't time for that. "Was he?"

"Randy? No," Warren said. "Who told you that?"

"I heard it through the grapevine." I turned into the parking lot of the bakery I'd gotten the cupcakes from. J's Bakery was in Elk Grove Village and had some of the tastiest cakes in town. They weren't the famous downtown cake girls, but they had been in business for nearly a hundred years. There was something about good old-fashioned baking that appealed to both me and Felicity.

"I don't know what grapevine you're tuned in to, but Randy did not blackmail me. To begin with, I haven't done anything worth blackmailing over. Unless you were thinking about the money I offered him to go into rehab for his gambling addiction. Pepper, I even offered to send him back to school once he got his addiction under control."

"So he had no reason to blackmail you . . ."

"He had no reason. I swear."

"Maybe you should have your lawyer tell the police that," I suggested.

"I did." He sounded upset. "They asked if I had proof. I don't know what kind of proof they wanted me to have. I don't make a habit out of recording conversations."

"Did you look up rehab places on the Internet? Or

maybe offer to pay his tuition at a certain school? Have them track your Internet searches. That's proof."

"I can't, Pepper. I have financially sensitive corporate information on my computer. There's a certain trust factor I have to maintain with my clients. If anyone even hinted that I would share that information with the cops, I wouldn't be able to do business."

"What about the business of proving your innocence?"

"Is that what this is about? Are you thinking I had something to do with Randy's death?"

"Let's just say that, for Felicity's sake, I hope not," I said. "She's my only sister. I don't want to see her hurt."

"I love Felicity," Warren insisted. "I wouldn't do anything to jeopardize our relationship."

"Not even pay off a blackmailer?" I turned off my car and sat in the parking lot in front of J's Bakery and studied the cakes in the window.

"Pepper, I swear—"

"What if we have the engagement party in Rosemont?" I asked, changing the subject. The man could swear he was innocent until he turned blue in the face. It wouldn't convince me I should believe him. Especially if the cops didn't believe him.

"Rosemont would be fine, too." Warren blew out a long breath. "Whatever Felicity wants. Okay?"

"Okay. Bye, Warren."

"Good-bye, Pepper."

I hung up and frowned at my steering wheel. Innocent

or not, Warren's proclamations didn't mean the police would stop suspecting him. The police needed evidence of his innocence that would stand up in court before they stopped. I needed them to stop. Preferably before Felicity married Warren and had a baby. I didn't want my niece or nephew having to go to prison on visiting day to meet their dad.

Chapter 11

"I'm serious, Pepper," Mom said. "You can't work from that tiny apartment of yours. You have to have a place where clients would feel comfortable meeting you."

"I'll meet them at Starbucks or Panera."

"Coffee shops and restaurants?" Mom looked horrified as she paused in her clothes folding. The towels had gone from a tangled pile to a neat stack of perfect squares.

"People do it all the time—especially if they are small business owners . . . like me." I twirled my coffee cup. It was Thursday morning. One of the perks of being self-employed was the ability to stop by and have coffee with my mom any day of the week.

"It doesn't seem appropriate," Mom said. "You have to be aware of your image when it comes to your own event planning. You no longer have a full marketing crew or corporate brand to back you up." She placed the stack of towels on the counter and dumped the load of clean whites on the table to be folded next.

I winced at her words. It wasn't as if her piano room in the basement would create the image she spoke of, either. "Mom, I'm fine living on my own. Really. All it will take is one or two well-placed events and I will open an office space. Okay?"

"You won't have to open an office space." Mom frowned and folded one of Dad's T-shirts with military precision. "I have a nice office space right here that you can use."

"I came over to talk engagement party." I sat at the small table in the basement laundry room. It smelled of dryer sheets and fabric softener. "Warren told me that money is no object, but that doesn't help me with the budget. I feel funny spending a lot of money without any set budget. What are your thoughts?"

"I thought your father and I were paying for the engagement party." Mom narrowed her eyes at me. "We've saved for years not only to put you both through school, but to pay for your weddings, too."

"Oh, sweet." I sat back. "But from my perspective, you might as well use it all on Felicity. I don't see a man in my life anytime soon—if ever."

"We will spend equally," Mom insisted as she folded the last of the T-shirts and started on the socks.

"Fine, but don't say I didn't warn you." I sipped coffee

and did my best to change the subject. "So what is your budget?"

The amount she so proudly gave me made me flinch. It would cover half the venue in Rosemont and an eighth of the Chicago venue. Rosemont it was. As long as Mom didn't ask for receipts, I would talk to Warren about paying the bills. I hated to make my parents feel bad. They really did work hard and save as much as possible. Felicity and I didn't care if we had simple parties in the warm atmosphere of the home we grew up in, but I know a man of Warren's stature demanded more than that.

It was a fine line to walk between budget and expectation. It was also something that I was good at doing.

"All right." I took my planner out of the large leather tote I carried and wrote a budget amount at the top. "I will need a list of people you want to invite. The numbers will help determine venue size."

Mom paired socks and flipped them together. "I have no idea how many people Warren's parents would like to invite. Warren gave me his mother's phone number and I've left two messages, but she has yet to return my calls."

"You and Felicity should meet with Warren's mom and have a get-to-know-you lunch."

"I'm sure that would be helpful." Mom took the clothes upstairs. I followed her. "Felicity hasn't even met his parents."

I leaned against the frame of the door to Mom and Dad's bedroom and watched her carefully put the clothes in drawers. Mom was so different than me. I generally shoved my clothes in whatever space they fit into. Mom always had a place for everything and everything in its place.

Dust never settled in Mom's house. Their bedroom always smelled like my Dad's aftershave and clean sheets. "She hasn't met his parents? That seems kind of weird, doesn't it?"

"Not really." Mom shrugged. "Felicity tells me that Warren thought introducing her to his parents sooner would have given away his secret."

"Seriously? Doesn't that bug her?"

"Listen up, kiddo, Warren Evans is the man your sister wants to marry." Mom turned on me, her gaze fierce. "You will support her in this."

I straightened up. It was habit really. Whenever Mom gave you "the look," you knew to take notice. "I simply don't understand his reasons for keeping these things from her, that's all."

"Warren's reasons are fine with Felicity and that's all that matters. I don't want to hear any more negative talk from you. It makes you sound jealous and petty."

"I'm not jealous." I drew my eyebrows together. "Really, I worry for her. That's all."

"If you love her, then you will take care not to let her become aware of your concerns. Felicity is the happiest I've ever seen her. I won't have anyone take that away from her."

I swallowed my reply and simply nodded. Mom was

right. It appeared I would be on my own with my investigation. To keep Felicity happy, I was even more determined than ever to find out who killed the janitor. "I understand."

"Good." Mom nodded. "Now are you staying for dinner?"

* * *

My talk with Mom only strengthened my desire to get to the bottom of this murder. Don't get me wrong, I liked Warren. He paid me well and gave me the idea to start my own business. The problem—as I saw it—was that as long as the investigation hung over their relationship, my sister would never be safe.

Since Mom would hear no more of my reservations, I took it upon myself to press Detective Murphy for more information. When he called me, I jumped at the chance to speak to him face-to-face.

"Thanks for coming down, Ms. Pomeroy." Detective Murphy sat at his desk. "You didn't have to. A simple phone call would have done it."

Detective Murphy wore a white shirt, a green striped tie, and black pants. I liked the fact that he wore a white T-shirt under his dress shirt. Not too many men wore T-shirts under dress shirts anymore. I liked that it gave the shirt a cleaner look. For an old guy, Detective Murphy was okay in my mind.

"I prefer to visit in person." I leaned toward him from

my place on the orange plastic chair in front of his desk. "You said the coroner determined a time of death for Mr. Stromer?"

"It's approximate, but yes, we have the window of time during which his death occurred," Detective Murphy said. "So tell me if you can what time you arrived at the airport?"

"It was around four P.M.," I said. "Jimmy should have it in his gate logs. They checked my ID before I was allowed into the airport."

"I'll check the logs later," he said. "For now give me your best version of the time frame."

"Okay." I sat back and held up my hand, marking each point on a finger. "I arrived after four P.M. My ID was checked and then Jimmy called Jeb Donaldson. I waited until Jeb got there and checked my ID again."

"How long did that take?"

"I don't know. Fifteen minutes or so? I remember that I'd been running a bit late and their delay at the gate had me worried about how much time I had left to get my decorating done before Felicity was supposed to arrive. Warren had asked her to come out after she got off work at five P.M."

"What time did you get to the hangar?" His hound dog eyes were flat and calm.

"You know, I don't have a watch."

"Estimate."

"Okay, well then, probably four twenty—if you

account for the delay at the gate and then five minutes to find the right hangar."

"Who was the first person you saw?" He wrote notes on a pad of yellow legal paper.

"Daniel Frasier, the pilot. He came out and offered to carry my potted palm into the hangar and show me around." I hadn't thought about the fact that Daniel would also be a suspect. In fact, he might be a better candidate than Warren.

"Was Frasier with you the entire time?"

"Well, no." I chewed on my bottom lip. "Let's see . . . he helped me bring the palm into the plane and showed me the interior."

"Was anyone else there when he did this?"

"Yes, Laura Snow, the flight attendant, was there as well, but they both left me while I decorated the interior. I have no idea what time that was or for how long. All I know is that I was on a deadline and I had a lot I wanted to do to create the perfect atmosphere."

"But you said your sister was to arrive by five P.M. Is that correct?" Detective Murphy looked at me over the top of his reading glasses.

"No, she was leaving work at five. She works in Des Plaines near O'Hare Airport. So you need to figure in extra time with traffic, she would most likely get there between five twenty and five forty. This means I couldn't have been decorating for more than forty-five minutes."

"So you were done decorating around five P.M."

"Give or take." I nodded and smoothed the pleats in my skirt. I had a meeting with the venue manager for Felicity's engagement party. So I was dressed professionally in a tan midcalf-length pleated skirt and a cream and tan sweater over a crisp white shirt. It made my orangered hair and blue eyes stand out.

"What do you consider give or take? Roughly? I want to clarify the timeline," he said as he made notes.

"Okay, well, give or take ten minutes," I said. "I'm terrible at estimating time. Ask anyone. I'm notoriously early or late—never on time."

"Maybe you need a watch."

"Maybe."

His dark gaze showed a hint of humor for the first time. "Who did you see after that?"

"I exited the plane and Daniel gave me a quick tour of the exterior—well, the safe zones anyway. I wasn't supposed to go past the wing. Wait—he did that before I decorated." I frowned. "I mixed that up. He took me on a tour inside and out—even showed me where the bathrooms were, all before I decorated."

"So he showed you the bathroom before you decorated. Did you go inside?"

"No."

"Did he go inside the restroom?"

"No, he simply pointed it out. Then I went back inside the plane and decorated." I threaded my fingers together nervously. How could I have mixed that up?

"Okay, so Frasier showed you the outside of the plane

and pointed out the restrooms, then you went into the plane and decorated. Correct?"

"Yes." I nodded. "When I came out, I was looking for Laura, the flight attendant. I didn't see her—but I did see Daniel in the cockpit."

"That fits with his statement," Detective Murphy muttered. "Did you find Laura?"

"No, I thought maybe she was in the bathroom, so I went in and called her name."

"Was the deceased inside at that time?"

I chewed on my lip. "Yes, but I thought he was passed out. I mean, he looked a little blue but some people turn green when they are drunk." I shrugged. "Green, blue, they are pretty close. So I was about to shake him and tell him he needed to leave when Warren opened the door a crack and let me know Felicity was coming through the gate."

"So you left the dead man and watched your sister's proposal, drank champagne, and waved them good-bye— letting everyone leave—knowing there was a dead guy in the bathroom?" He raised one gray eyebrow and gave me a look like I was about the biggest idiot he'd ever known.

"I didn't think he was dead," I defended my actions. "I've never seen a real-life dead person, except at funerals, and they don't count."

"So you thought he was passed out and didn't think to tell anyone there was a passed-out *man* in the ladies' room?" He crossed his arms and leaned back in his chair.

I tried not to twitch. "I was caught up in the excitement of my sister's big day. I didn't think it was a big deal. After all, Laura and I were the only women in the hangar that I knew of and we were both busy. I didn't think that a passed-out man would disturb anyone. Besides, for all I know, he died while Warren was proposing." I fished for a timeline on the janitor's death. Detective Murphy ignored me.

"When did you realize he was dead?"

"After they left, I went to collect my bags and I remembered the man in the bathroom. I called 911. The dispatcher took my information and told me to call airport security. After I talked to Jeb on the phone, I figured I'd better check on the drunk guy. I mean, if he got up and left, then there was nothing I could do, but if he was still in the stall, I could at least stay with him until the police came."

"So you went back into the bathroom with a possible drunk that you didn't know and didn't take anyone with you?"

Now he did make me feel foolish. "Yeah, I guess that wasn't very smart." I wasn't about to mention that I was afraid the drunk guy would leave before the police got there. "He was drunk, right? I could outrun him if he tried anything."

"When did you realize he was dead?"

"He was still in the same spot when I went back inside. His position in the bathroom stall looked painful, so I went to shake him. I thought if I could get him out of there and maybe at least get him flat on the floor, it would help. I used a mop handle to poke him . . ." I shuddered. "He was cold and stiff."

"We have in our records that you called 911 at six thirty P.M."

"That sounds about right." I clenched my hands together.

"Evans's jet was cleared to takeoff at six fifteen P.M. How do you account for the difference?"

"I went out to watch them take off and see if Cesar was in place to take the appropriate footage."

"I see."

"I could not have killed him between six fifteen and six thirty," I said. "He was too cold."

"He was killed earlier." Detective Murphy didn't look up from his notes. "But you could have hid evidence or tried to clean up." This time he glanced up and pinned me with his brown cop's gaze.

"I didn't," I said, pulling back my emotions. "I called 911 and was advised to call airport security. I looked up the number and gave Jeb Donaldson a call. It was when Jeb got there that we determined the guy was actually dead."

"Where was Evans during all this?" he asked, his gaze going back to the notes in front of him.

"In the plane, flying to a romantic destination with my sister."

"Where was Evans when you were decorating the plane?" He said it slowly as if I were a small child.

"I don't know." I unclenched my hands and leaned forward. "Is that when the janitor was killed? Does Warren not have an alibi?"

He closed his eyelids for a moment and then opened them. "Do you have an alibi?"

"Yes, I was in the plane decorating it." I sat back.

"Was there anyone else with you at the time?"

"Well, Laura was there for a while . . ." I pursed my lips and frowned. "She must have left because I didn't see her when I went looking for Cesar. Maybe she was outside supervising the luggage guy. I don't know. I found Cesar and pulled him into the plane." I leaned forward. "We put him in the airplane toilet with a view of the cabin so that he could film in secret. Ingenious, wasn't it?"

"Brilliant." He said it with a flat tone as he wrote on his note pad. "Did you see Evans at all during this time?"

"No . . . I imagine he was in his office finishing up business things."

"Business things?" Detective Murphy asked.

"I don't know, maybe e-mails and stuff like that. What does an executive do while he waits for his girlfriend to show up so he can propose?"

"I doubt he checks his e-mail," Detective Murphy muttered.

I pursed my lips and raised the right corner. This wasn't going very well at all. I made it sound even more likely that Warren could have done it. My gaze landed on a framed picture of a woman around my age on

Detective Murphy's desk. I reached over and picked it up. "Is this your wife?" I tilted my head and tried not to sound judgmental. I mean May-December marriages happened all the time. Then again, maybe I had her age wrong. Maybe she was older than me.

"That's my daughter, Emily." He took the frame from my hand. "She's about your age."

"How do you know my age?" I asked.

"It's in Vandall's report."

"Oh, right." I looked around and tried to breathe through the uncomfortable silence.

"You kind of remind me of her." Detective Murphy leaned back in his chair.

"I do?"

"Yes, you do." He crossed his arms. "Too curious for your own good."

"What does she do?"

"She's a nurse anesthetist, like her mother." There was a glint of pride in his eye.

"Wow, she must be very smart."

"And lovely." He straightened the picture.

"And lovely." I had to give him that because she was. "Does she live at home?"

"No." He shook his head. "She lives in California with her boyfriend."

"Wow, that has to be hard for you and your wife."

"Her mom died a few years back," he said gruffly. "Cancer."

I put my hand to my mouth and felt a rush of heat from embarrassment. "I'm so sorry."

"It's okay. It was years ago." He picked up his pen and concentrated on his notes.

I knew when a subject was politely closed. So I reached down and picked up my purse. "What about the video-tapes around the hangar?"

"What about them?" That caught his attention.

"Do they show that I was on the plane doing the decorating?"

"There are no security tapes inside the hangars," he said. "You do not have an alibi."

I frowned. "Neither does Daniel or Laura."

"Daniel claims to have been going over his preflight checklist. Since it has time slots, the lists should verify where he was and when. Laura was speaking to Jeb Donaldson. They alibied each other. That leaves you and Warren Evans."

"And Daniel," I stated. "He could have forged his lists. He's a more likely suspect than I am."

Detective Murphy folded his big calloused hands on the top of his notes. "I can't discuss details of the investigation. I think you know that, Ms. Pomeroy."

I nodded. "But you want me to tell you everything I know."

"Yes, I do," he said. "It's my job to investigate a crime. Not yours. I don't know what you do for a living, Ms. Pomeroy—"

"I'm an event planner." I raised my chin. "I'm opening

my own business to plan proposals for men who want to do something special for their ladies. I'm calling it Personal . . . no Perfect Proposals."

"Sounds like you have it all planned out."

"I do." I stepped away from the plastic chair. "I plan on doing engagement parties as well as the proposals. If you ever know someone who wants to propose, send him my way. I promise to put together something perfect for his soon-to-be bride."

"And if she says no?"

"Then I'll be there with a sad sports movie and a case of beer. I know how to plan things, Detective Murphy."

"I see that. Let's hope you didn't turn that talent to murder . . ."

Chapter 12

"What about the dozens of people at the airport?" Felicity asked me. "Why are they concentrating on you and Warren? There were so many people there that day."

I fiddled with the brochures of venues I'd brought with me to the coffee shop. "I think they've spoken to everyone they can find. Jimmy tells me that several of the people who were at the airport are away on business. It's an airport after all. Now, which venue would you prefer?" I pushed the brochures toward her.

"I can't stop thinking of that poor man and his family. Are you certain that he will be buried before we have this party?"

My sister wrinkled her small forehead in concern. Her

blond hair hung in long, soft curls today. She wore a work outfit of a navy pencil skirt and cream-colored sweater set. Her heels were gorgeous three-inch spectator pumps in navy and cream.

She always did know how to dress. Meanwhile, I had been scouring prop houses and flea markets for props for the party. That meant I was currently dressed in dark jeans and a tucked-in cobalt blue blouse with dust smudges on the collar. My hair had a few cobwebs stuck in it. Next time I went looking for props, I had to remember to wear a head scarf to protect my hair.

"Detective Murphy assured me that it would be fine if we have this party. As long as no one goes out of town on business, we're okay. Now, there is this lovely place in Rosemont." I pushed the first brochure toward her. "Then this penthouse in downtown Chicago—which may actually be closer to Mom and Dad's."

"I like the penthouse." Felicity surprised me. "Look at that view. It would be as if we brought the families into the plane with us." She sighed over the brochure that showed the Chicago skyline at night.

"The penthouse it is," I said. "Mom and Dad want to pay for the party."

"Oh, no." Felicity looked at me with horror on her face. Her eyes went wide, her eyebrows rose, and her pink mouth made a little O. "They can't afford this place in Rosemont, let alone the penthouse. Forget it. We can have a small affair in their backyard."

I leaned my elbows on the table and rested my chin in my palm. "Mom doesn't know how much these venues cost. I won't tell her, either. Warren gave me cart blanche for this affair. I will see that Mom and Dad get minimal bills so they can feel as if they paid. The rest will go to Warren."

"Isn't that lying to them?" Felicity studied the brochures. "Or is it only a slight omission?" She lifted her gaze and pinned me with it. "In my opinion, not billing Mom and Dad for the entire affair would be as bad as Warren keeping his wealth from me."

Okay, so she had a point. Maybe Warren had a purpose for his lie. Maybe he wasn't a bad guy after all. It didn't mean I didn't need to solve this case. In fact, it made it worse. If Warren was a bad guy, it would be simple to turn him in and be done. But everything about this was more complicated. Even good guys went to jail sometimes. Felicity might still end up married to a felon. I could not let that happen.

"Okay, yes, I deserved that. I will admit that Warren's lie was within reason. I think I was mad because I fell for it. I had no idea he was so rich." I leaned back. "You know I pride myself on being able to read people well. It's terrible when I fail so miserably."

"Don't worry." Felicity patted my hand. "Warren did an excellent job of hiding his wealth. I'm sure you'll get back into the swing of things soon."

"Right. Now, back to the party," I said. "Rooftop

penthouse with a *Great Gatsby* theme? I mean, a 1920s biplane party. What do you think?"

"I think it's awesome."

"Good." I clapped my hands. "Then it's settled. Now what dress are you going to wear?"

"Mom is taking me shopping." Felicity rolled her eyes. "I hope she lets me wear something pretty and not anything childish."

"Oh, you will always be Mom and Dad's little girl. Remember, you don't put Baby in a corner?" I smiled.

"You are far from that movie's weirdo older sister." Felicity squeezed my hands.

"Because she had black hair, right?" I laughed. Meanwhile my mind raced to figure out how to decorate the venue. There would be so much to do. Next I needed to get some business cards printed up, because if the party went as well as I planned, then I might be able to pick up some business.

Wouldn't that be wonderful?

* * *

"Thank you for meeting me here," I said to Officer Vandall. "I bought you a large coffee, and these donuts are for you." I handed him the cup and the box of fresh Krispie Kremes. "I don't know what you take in your coffee so I have creamer and sugar." I gave him a small bag filled with accompaniments.

"Thanks." Officer Vandall put the donuts in the

passenger seat across from him. "What can I do for you, Ms. Pomeroy? I know you didn't ask me out here to bring me donuts."

Out here was the Walmart parking lot in Wheeling, a village close to the airport. I knew Officer Vandall was on patrol today. I'd called the station and asked for him. It wasn't that hard to track him down, and I hoped a bribe would work for him as well as it did with Jimmy.

He tugged his sunglasses down and eyed my chest. "I'm not much of a donut guy, but my partner is so these will come in handy."

I smiled and leaned onto his open car window and twirled the end of my hair. If donuts didn't work, perhaps flirting would. Although I wasn't the best at flirting, I'd recently read a book that said twirling your hair was a distinct sign of interest. "I've been so worried about that poor man whose body I discovered at the airport. I never did hear—did he die of a heart attack? Was there something I could have done to save him?" I had always been good at fake tears. It was my only talent besides party planning. I squeezed out a fat tear and quivered my bottom lip.

"Hey now, no tears," Officer Vandall said and put up his hand as if that would stop me. "You could not have saved him."

"But I know CPR." I raised the pitch of my voice and let the waterworks fly. "I'm sure I could have saved him. I just . . . I can't sleep . . . If he had a heart attack, I could have done CPR . . ."

"Stop crying." Officer Vandall opened the car door. "He did not die of a heart attack."

"Oh, my God! Was he choking? Because I'm also trained in the Heimlich maneuver. I should have tried to sweep his throat and then put my knee in his back." I put my hands over my face and let my shoulders shake. "I knew it. I knew his death was all my fault."

Officer Vandall got out of the car and patted me on the back awkwardly. "No, no, he did not die of choking. Trust me. You could not have saved him."

"But I didn't see any wounds like bullet holes or knife marks from stabbing. It means he had to die of something I could have saved him from," I wailed and threw myself in his arms. I rested my forehead on his shoulder and noted that his gun belt stuck out kind of far. "It's all my fault that he's dead, isn't it?"

"No." He continued to pat me awkwardly. "No. He was murdered, Ms. Pomeroy."

"I don't believe you." I grabbed his shirt and sobbed into his chest. "There were no murder wounds. It had to be a heart attack."

"No, no, it didn't." He stepped back and held me out at arm's length. I know my face was red, I sniffled, and my eyes watered like leaky faucets. "Look." He dug a facial tissue out of his pocket, handed it to me, and then glanced around to see if anyone could hear. "I'm going to tell you something, but you have to promise not to tell anyone I told you."

I hiccupped and blew my nose into the tissue. "Okay . . ."

"I will deny ever saying anything, do you understand?"

I nodded and for good measure squeezed out a couple more tears. "I feel so guilty." I swiped at my eyes.

"The guy overdosed," he said. "Not your fault."

"But, but I didn't see any pills or anything . . . if they overdose, shouldn't they foam at the mouth or something? Oh, my goodness, were there pills in the toilet? Was there something I missed?" I wailed.

"No, no." He pulled me in and patted me on the back. "No, he was murdered. Someone injected him with a drug that stopped his heart. Trust me, no amount of CPR could have saved him."

"No?" I said softly and sniffled.

"No. The guy was long gone by the time you found him."

I stepped back and wiped my nose. "But Detective Murphy made it sound as if he died while I was at the airport. He questioned my timeline and everything."

"Murphy is doing his job." Officer Vandall patted my arm. "Timelines are part of any case. Trust me. You are not a person of interest in this investigation. Okay?"

"Oh, okay." I blew my nose loud.

"Feel better now?"

"Yes," I said and sent him a watery smile. "Thank you. Maybe I can sleep tonight."

"Of course you can sleep, jeez." He put his sunglasses back on and looked around. "Stop crying, okay?"

"Okay." I dried my eyes with the tissue. "Thanks for your help."

"You're welcome," he said, his gaze still on the surroundings. I did my best not to look over my shoulder even though I wanted to. I needed him to continue to believe I was thinking only of what I could have done to save the janitor. "Look, I've got to get back to my patrol. My partner is waiting for me at the station." He raised my chin with his gloved finger. "Stop worrying, okay?"

"Okay," I whispered. "Thank you."

He got in his squad car. "No problem. If you think of anything, you call me. Okay?"

"Okay," I agreed and waved as he put his car in reverse and took off.

It never paid to smirk, no matter how badly you wanted to. I got into my own car and touched up my makeup. So Stromer was injected with a drug that stopped his heart. What kind of drug would do that, and more important, who had access to such a drug?

I put on fresh lipstick and glanced at my appearance in my rearview mirror. Having fair skin was a hassle most of the time, but there were days when it worked to your advantage. Today was one of those days. The splotchiness that came with tears helped them look authentic. I was lucky in that the red faded as fast as the fake tears.

I put my car in gear and pulled out of the parking lot in the opposite direction of Officer Vandall. I headed toward Chicago. I had a downtown lunch meeting with Felicity's venue. It was time to sign a contract and do a tasting. I had mentioned the 1920s airplane theme. The hotel event manager loved the idea. At first she had suggested historic airline food as appetizers. I declined. This was a high-end engagement party, not a place for bags of peanuts, no matter how ironic they may seem.

Chapter 13

"Hi, I'm Pepper Pomeroy. I'm planning the Evans-Pomeroy engagement party," I said to an assistant in the hospitality management offices at the W Hotel downtown Chicago.

"Ah, yes," the assistant said. "Amanda is expecting you. Please have a seat. She will be with you momentarily." She waved toward the chairs lined up against the wall.

I took a seat and pulled out my phone. Today I was dressed in a dark blue pencil skirt, a lighter blue button-down blouse with French cuffs, and a white cardigan. I had unbuttoned the top button for my visit with Officer Vandall.

Who knew tears were the best course of action with

him? I was banking on the donuts. Too bad I didn't keep them for myself. Ah, well, it was probably best that I didn't. No one could eat only one Krispy Kreme, and they had a terrible tendency to go straight to my bum.

I considered Googling "what drugs can stop a human heart" on my phone, but then I paused. What if Detective Murphy was able to get a warrant for my Internet records? So, no, I would have to go to the library or use one of my friends' computers.

"Ms. Pomeroy?"

I looked up to see a shorter, round-faced blonde coming my way with her hand outstretched. "Yes." I stood.

"I'm Amanda Kozlowski," she said. "I'm your contract manager. We have the venue reserved for the Evans-Pomeroy party in thirty days."

"Yes." I nodded and pulled out a piece of paper from my day planner. "I have some menu ideas based on 1920s dinner party menus."

"On paper?" she asked as I handed her a copy of my favorite menu.

"Yes, how else would I give it to you?"

"Oh, we are all high-tech now. You need to get yourself a tablet as well as a smart phone. The hotel has an app that will let you upload menus so that the cook can see your ideas and price a variety of your choices."

"Oh, right." I made a note in my planner to buy a tablet.

"Come on. I booked a tasting room for you, if you would follow me." She walked down the hallway in four-inch platform shoes made of hot pink patent leather. The heels worked for her. Even with the four inches, she only came up to my eye level. I followed behind. My own shoes were two-inch kitten heels.

She was very stylish in her black sweater dress with a body-conscious fit. Her hair was cut in an asymmetrical bob. Her jewelry was chunky stone and over the top in design. "Second door on the right." She opened a glass door into a small room with one glass wall that over-looked the Chicago skyline. There was a small round table and four chairs inside. "Please have a seat."

I sat so that I could see out the window. It was a stunning view, and I was certain the venue would be perfect for that airplane feel.

"I see you have nine courses listed. Did you want a sit-down meal or buffet?" She looked at me from over the top of the paper. Amanda had round features and blue eyes. Her skin was as flawless as silk. I felt frumpy with my orange hair and freckles. I smoothed my skirt and leaned forward.

"I thought we could have mini courses come through as finger foods. The idea being wine and cocktails all night. If you notice there is a wine with each menu."

"Yes, I see. You start with tuna tartare and Riesling."

"I was thinking small—flavorful bites for each course brought out in fifteen-minute intervals with mini wineglasses."

"Sounds different." Amanda put down the sheet. "I think that Chief Michael might be up to the idea. If you don't mind, I'll take him this menu. Give me five minutes. There is coffee in the corner. Please help yourself."

She left me in the room. I got up and walked over to where she had pointed and found a coffeemaker. There was a silver tray with a wide variety of drinks from coffee to teas. I pulled out a bold coffee, followed the instructions, and moments later had a large cup of black coffee with a dash of half-and-half. I took a sip and looked out the window for inspiration.

A bank of soft clouds floated by the window. I was on the thirtieth floor. The hotel faced east to west. The skyline was on the west side. The lake on the east. The penthouse venue offered views of both the lake and the city. It would be perfect.

I made a note to myself to research jazz music to add to the ambience of the party. My cell phone rang and I picked up.

"Felicity?"

"Hi, Pepper. Warren and I were able to move our schedules around. Is it okay if we come by for the tasting?"

I turned to the room. There were four chairs at the table. "Yes, please, I would love to have your input. Do you know where to go?"

"Warren knows—here, I'll put you on speaker."

"Hi, Pepper, we're almost there." Warren's voice rang through the phone. "I know Amanda, we did a few fundraisers at the W. Tell her we'll be right over."

"Will do." I couldn't help the smile in my voice. Their

happiness was contagious. How could I have ever doubted Warren? I guess I had Detective Murphy to credit with my change of heart. When he suspected me of murder based on my circumstances and lack of alibi, he showed me how easy it was to misunderstand a person's situation.

All I really wanted was for Felicity to be this happy always. It's why I was determined to help find the killer. I never wanted there to be a reason—even a false one—for my baby sister to lose the love of her life.

I dialed Amanda's number. I know she kept her cell phone with her. I'd seen it on her belt.

"This is Amanda, how can I help you?"

"Hi, Amanda, this is Pepper Pomcroy. My sister, Felicity, called and she and Warren Evans are on their way in to help with the tasting."

"No problem, I'll have the server set the table for three."

Felicity and Warren arrived as the server finished setting the table. He had placed three settings of 1920s vintage china and glassware on the table. It looked like we would be able to pick china as well as the tasty dishes.

"Thank you so much for doing this." Felicity rushed up and gave me a kiss and a hug.

Warren looked flushed and happy. They were both dressed for work. Felicity had on a cute little ice blue suit with a full skirt that came to her knees. Warren wore an Italian-cut business suit of charcoal gray with a blue shirt that matched his eyes.

"It's my pleasure," I said and returned her affection. "Sit. Tell me what you think of the china."

"Oh, my goodness, it's all so lovely." Felicity sat in the chair Warren pulled out for her. He pulled mine out as well and I was astonished at his manners. A man with manners was difficult to find in this day and age.

"The china patterns are all 1920s," Amanda said. "Original to the hotel at the time."

"I love the graphic feel of the pattern on the right," I said. "What do you think, Warren?"

"I think the idea of a Roaring Twenties party is fabulous. You really have a knack for these things, Pepper."

"Thanks." The heat of a blush rushed up my cheeks. "I'm taking your advice and starting my own business. I'm going to plan wedding proposals and the engagement party."

"Oh, my gosh, that's perfect," Felicity said, her blue eyes sparkling. "Be sure and keep everything you did for mine as an example."

"I plan on it, if that's okay with you both . . ."

"Oh, of course, it is," Felicity gushed. "Isn't it, Warren?"

"It was my idea," he said. "Do you have a business plan?"

"I've been working on one," I said with pride.

"Good, when you're done, send me a copy. I want to invest in your company."

"What?" I sat back.

"I'll go over the plan and help you tweak it, and then

I want to be a silent partner. I believe in you, Pepper," he said as he put a napkin on his lap. "I have the ability to fund good talent when I see it. Let me partner with you."

"But—"

"Give me two years," he said. "If you're sick of me—"

"Or you're sick of me . . ."

"Then you can buy me out. Agreed?" He held out his hand.

"What if I can't buy you out?" I drew my eyebrows together. Worry wrapped itself through my mind. I wanted to do this for me. I didn't want to owe anyone. But then again, I had been looking at the initial numbers on the business plan and a fresh flow of start-up cash would really help.

"You will be able to buy me out," he said with confidence and motioned with his hand. "I would never support a business I wasn't a hundred percent sold on. Now shake and we can get back to the tasting."

I shook. Felicity's joy washed over me. Warren had believed in me even when I doubted his sincerity. He had that unique ability to start over fresh. I pulled my hand from his warm one and watched as the waiter came in with covered dishes on a room service cart.

Was it possible that he was doing this to throw me off his trail as a suspect? I mean, I was indebted to him now. How could I turn on him if my investigation showed me Warren was the killer? I mentally shook off the thought. If I were to find out that Warren was the killer, I would still tell the police no matter what. In the meantime,

Warren's financial help gave me hope for myself and my ability to take charge of my own future. From now on, I was the boss. My business would succeed or fail based on my own abilities. For the first time in a long time I could feel real hope and confidence blossom in my chest. I could do this. I really could.

Chapter 14

Felicity and Warren had loved the menu I'd created. The chef had outdone himself as well with tiny tasty bites of an actual feast and the wines that matched.

I sat in my apartment and worked on my business plan. The sounds of a group laughing and coming out of the bar on the corner caught my attention. I looked out to see some of Bobby's work friends going inside. Bobby's favorite drinking buddy, Harry, held the door for the rest of the gang.

It felt a little odd not to rush down to meet them. I dropped the sheer curtain that covered the old windows on my apartment and resolutely went back to my desk.

The business plan was nearly finished. I had done a

lot of work on it. Part of my event planning/hospitality major in college was to come up with an accurate business plan. At the time I'd written it for a small children's party planner business.

Proposal planning was close to the same thing—minus the magicians and clowns. I had spent an hour online researching statistics of how many people in the area marry every year and extrapolated for how many proposals I would be able to plan. My overhead would be low. With a smart phone and a tablet, I could plan pretty much anything from my car.

The new social media Pintrest was a big help. People pinned pictures to a wide variety of boards. The first thing I could do was research each potential bride and see what kinds of things she pinned. It was a great way to determine her design style and incorporate her favorite things into the proposal plan.

A good business plan also accounted for any unexpected expenses in the first year, and from what I could tell, I would be able to make a go of this business without too much of Warren's money. I wanted to keep the overhead low so that I could pay him back sooner rather than later. He was a nice guy, but my parents taught me that it was better to pay off loans as quickly as possible.

I put the last touches on the plan and printed out a copy for Warren. A glance at the clock told me it was 10 P.M. and the bar was probably starting to get rowdy. I thought of Bobby and how I'd left him. It had been hard to break up in front of Gage, but I knew I'd done the right thing.

The light on my phone blinked and I turned it on to see that I had a missed call. A quick check of the number told me it was Bobby who'd called. I deleted the message without listening. Knowing Bobby, he would remind me of a time when he had done something out of the ordinary—like when he had won money at the casino in Des Plaines and had used it to pay for a romantic weekend getaway. In Bobby's mind, a happy weekend four years ago was proof he loved me.

I blew out a long breath and went to bed. Bobby could wait another day.

* * *

The next morning I stood in my living room and listened to the Metra train rattle by. I had bed hair. I know this because I always had bed hair in the morning, but this time I didn't care. In fact, to celebrate breaking up with Bobby for good, I stayed in my favorite pink and white striped pajamas. It was 8 A.M., and I was eager to continue making changes in my life.

The first thing I needed to do was to box up Bobby's stuff and put it out in the hall. Not for the first time I was glad I'd insisted on living alone. Bobby had tried for years to get me to let him move in with me. It's why he had so much stuff here. Looking back, I realized my reluctance should have been a real clue. My excuse was my parents would never forgive me. Frankly, I have no clue if that were true or not. For all I knew, they thought Bobby and I had been living together for years.

I pulled up a big moving box, one of three I'd picked up at the storage unit shop and tossed Bobby's things inside. There was his collection of random CDs. They made a distinctive thunk in the bottom of the box. His beer-bottle-cap collection—all three jars' worth—made a satisfying clink and jingle as I placed them next to the CDs. Next came the collection of ball caps from every NASCAR race he'd ever been to see. I turned the corner to the next wall and pulled his game system off the shelf. He'd brought it in one night pronouncing he'd bought it for me to do workouts with . . . Then he'd proceeded to bring in a variety of his favorite games. Suddenly, the game system became his real reason to come over—that and the beer in my refrigerator.

It was hard to remember that there was a time when he was the star quarterback and I was his girl. In those days he'd put his letter jacket around my shoulders and I'd imagine we were Sandy and Danny from *Grease*. I thought we were destined to be together forever.

The games went into the box with a click and a snap. The controller was next. It was funny how he'd only bought one of those.

Then there was the framed picture of his dog. The photo of Bobby standing next to his truck and a handful of beer steins all got packed away, too. When the box was full, I pulled it out into the hallway and shut my door on it with a satisfying clap of my hands.

The next room was my bedroom. When I had moved in, I'd bought neutral bedding so that Bobby wouldn't feel as if he were sleeping in a girl's bed. I ripped that off with sadness and satisfaction. The bedding was a symbol of my life. I had sacrificed my own desires for Bobby and a dream that didn't happen. It was time to grow up and move on. My first stop—when I decided to get dressed and go out—would be to the bedding store. I was going to purchase whatever girlie bedding struck my fancy. Let freedom ring!

At that thought my cell phone rang. I whirled about in an effort to find it before it stopped. I found it under a stack of muscle magazines and hit the answer button. "Hello?"

"Pepper?"

"Yeah," I said as I frowned at the magazines. They had my address on them. I certainly didn't read them.

"It's Warren." He sounded tentative. "Are you doing okay?"

"Yes, hi, I'm fine." I tossed the magazines in the trash. "What can I do for you?"

"I have a client for Perfect Proposals," Warren announced.

My eyes widened and my heartbeat picked up. "Really? That's fabulous. Let me get my pen, I want to write the info in my desk planner."

I hurried over to my desk and sat down. I was surprised to see there were two pens left in my pen holder—a pink one and a blue one. The rest had been Bobby's and had gone in a box. I snatched the blue.

"Don't get too excited," Warren said. "It's for my friend Keith. He wants to propose to his girlfriend and I told him about you. The thing is this. He won't be able to pay for your services—only the props and venue and such. But he's willing to let you use him in your portfolio. How's that sound?"

I covered my disappointment quite nicely. "No problem. It would be great to have more work in my portfolio."

"That's the spirit." Warren's voice brightened. "Here's Keith's number. He has an interesting problem. When you solve this, he'll be thrilled."

I wrote down the phone number Warren gave me and hung up the phone. A quick look around my apartment and it became very clear to me that the place looked bare. Somehow in my enthusiasm to make my home appealing to Bobby, I had forgotten to make it appealing to me.

"Well, that's about to change," I muttered and stood. I grabbed another scrap of paper and made a list of things I needed to get the business off and running. A quick inventory showed I needed things like business cards, brochures, a website, a new computer, a new desk, a fax machine, and a color printer. I made one more turn about the place to ensure that everything Bobby was packed up and out in the hallway. Then I headed for the shower. If I was going to start the business off on the right foot, then

I needed to be sure I was showered, professionally dressed, and properly focused before I called my first client.

It was difficult to think like a professional when you had cobwebs in your hair.

Chapter 15

♂

"Warren tells me you are the best at this proposal planning thing." Keith Emry's voice was sincere.

"Let me assure you, Mr. Emry, that Perfect Proposals is here to help you give your lady a unique and romantic proposal. She will be thrilled with what we put together. Now, let's talk about your girlfriend. What's the favorite thing you like to do together?"

I opened my tablet and typed the heading "Personality" on the top of the notes section.

"Besides the obvious?" He chuckled and heat rushed over my cheeks when I realized what I had said.

"Yes." I cleared my throat. "What kinds of things do you do when you go out?" I typed a note to self to make a list of standard questions. Preferably ones that I had run past my mom, Felicity, and possibly Warren. I didn't want to make another mistake like that one.

"Amy and I love to scuba dive," Keith's voice rumbled through the phone. "We've taken dive trips to some of the best places, like the Great Barrier Reef."

"Wow, and she likes that?" I thought of that movie where the two divers were stranded in the ocean. Scary. I made another note to myself not to mention that thought.

"She loves it," he said. "But here's the thing, I want to propose here in Chicago. Amy wouldn't want to be anywhere else when I propose and I agree. It would be great if our family and friends would be waiting in the wings, like Warren did with you. I can see her wanting to squeal over everything with her friends."

"I'll do my best to elicit a squeal of delight out of her," I promised. "So the dive must take place here in Chicago."

"Yes."

"Great." It was October so a warm outside dive was out of the question. "Do you have those cold weather suits?"

"No, that's part of my problem. We only dive where it's warm, which is not Chicago."

"Oh," I chuckled, understanding his dilemma. "I see how it could be a problem to have a dive proposal here. Lake Michigan isn't exactly romantic diving. I'll work on that. Now, when it comes to colors, what are her favorites?"

"She loves pink. I think if she had it her way, the entire world would be pink. Then there's this dress she wears that is ruffled and sparkly."

"Okay." I drummed my fingers on the desk. "Does she like sunsets or sunrises?"

"Both because . . . they have pink in them."

"Right." I chewed on my bottom lip. "What kind of jewelry does she like? Silver or gold?"

"She likes gold. She says it goes with her tan skin and her blond hair. My girl is hot."

"Got it." I warmed to the enthusiasm in his tone. "Does she have a favorite drink?"

"Pink champagne."

"You're kidding me." I smiled when I said it so as not to offend him.

"Not kidding." I swear I could hear him shake his head. "She also likes stuffed animals, feather boas, sky-high heels, and anything that blings. One year for Christmas I got her one of those bedazzle machines."

"Let me guess, she loved it."

"Yes! Her girlfriends loved it, too. They made sparkly lamp shades and napkin holders and shoes and things I don't want to think about right now."

I smothered my laugh. My mom was big into the bedazzler as well. I still had four sweatshirts she had bedazzled to within an inch of their lives. Me, I liked sparkle when it was in the right place and the right time. "What about movies? What is her favorite movie?"

"You know what? She likes all those sappy Tom Hanks

movies. She and her girlfriends had a movie marathon sleepover last weekend when I had to go out of town for work. She kept texting me her favorite quotes starting with 'You've got mail . . .'

He sounded indulgently happy about her movie choices if not a little bit bemused. "Then there are all those Disney movies. She loves a happy ever after."

"Right." I typed "Disney princess" in the column. "Wow, okay." I looked at the descriptors and had no idea what I was going to come up with. "Well, Mr. Emry—"

"Call me Keith, please. With Warren engaged to your sister, we're practically family."

"Okay, Keith, it sounds like we have a real challenge on our hands, but I promise you I'll come up with something that incorporates everything you've talked about. Now, I also offer a package where I plan the engagement party as well as the proposal. No charge for you, of course, if I can use it for my portfolio."

"That would be perfect."

"Do you want the party immediately after the proposal or within a month?"

"As far as I'm concerned, there isn't any need to delay."

"Then I'll plan it for immediately following the proposal. Is there a family member with a birthday in the next month?"

"Why?"

"We can use a birthday party as an excuse to gather family and friends." That sounded good, I thought, and made a note.

"Um, sure, my friend Sam has a birthday the end of the month."

"Great, do you think Sam will let us use him as a ruse?"

"She would probably love it actually," Keith said.

"Oh, Sam as in Samantha." I made another note. "Even better, actually. A surprise party for a woman is more believable and opens up the venue possibilities. Now, if I could have her number, that would help. I need to have Sam's party seem as real as possible so that Amy doesn't ever suspect anything. We can't spoil our element of surprise, now can we?"

"No, I wouldn't want that," Keith said and gave me Sam's number. "You know, you are really good at this."

"Thanks." I tried not to show my panic at figuring out how to plan a proposal for a scuba diving girly girl in Chicago.

"Listen I know this other dude who wants to propose to his girlfriend in a way that will have her talking for years. Can I give him your number?"

"Yes, of course," I said and tried to suppress my glee. "Anything I can add to my portfolio would help."

"His name is Mike Keifer and be sure to charge him for your services. He can well afford it."

My heartbeat picked up as I wrote down Mike's name. It was one I'd seen in the society pages. If I could plan a Keifer proposal that got the whole city talking, then I would be on my way to establishing Perfect Proposals as the only place to go when you wanted to create an unforgettable experience for your lady love.

I hung up the phone and went straight to the Internet. Before Mike Keifer called, I was going to have to set my event-planning packages. The first step for doing that was to Google what the going rates were for high-end wedding planners. Then I'd try the low end and settle somewhere in between, factoring in my years of experience, forty percent for taxes, ten percent for insurance, and wow, there was a lot to consider when you started your own business.

* * *

"You should let your father look at your business plan," Mom announced. She had called and asked me to meet her for lunch at Portillo's "He's been a small-business owner his whole life. He knows a thing or two about it, you know."

I tried not to sigh, hiding my emotions by sipping my Pepsi. For October it was a bright, warm day. The sky was pure blue and we sat out on the patio, letting the sun shine on us. I wore a pale blue sweater set, a black pencil skirt, black tights, and booties. I'd gone into town this morning and handed my business plan off to Warren's secretary, then checked on table arrangements for Felicity's engagement party before meeting mom at the restaurant chain known for its hot dogs.

"I'm sure Dad has other things to do besides look over

my plan. Besides, it's not the same. I don't own a building and I don't have any employees."

"Not yet." Mom picked the onions off her hot dog. "But that doesn't mean you shouldn't plan for those things in the future."

"You know you can order your hot dog without onions," I pointed out for the hundredth time.

"It's easier to pick them off than to say everything but onions," she said and bit into a French fry. "Now tell me again what you're going to do with this scuba proposal thingie."

"I'm not sure yet." I bit into my hot dog and savored the warm, beefy juices. I liked my hot dogs with everything including sauerkraut and pickles. "I was thinking about doing something at the Shedd Aquarium. I have a call in to their business manager."

"What if you can't get them to let you plan something?"

"There's also this resort in Saint Charles with a heated pool that is indoor-outdoor. I could do some kind of under-the-sea theme . . . with mermaids and such."

"You used to love *The Little Mermaid* when you were a kid. You must have watched it fifty times. I'm surprised you didn't break the VCR tape."

That made me laugh. "She was the only Disney princess with red hair." I thought about it for a moment. "You know, she did collect baubles and such. Keith's girlfriend, Amy, likes all things girly so maybe we're on to something with the mermaid theme."

"You'd have to be careful that the party doesn't get too childish," Mom warned. "It could go wrong very fast."

My eyes grew wide. "It's not like I'm going to have Disney posters and plastic rings."

Mom laughed. "Thank goodness you are good at this stuff. If I tried to plan a mermaid theme, I'm certain the party would go on one of those reality shows where the designer has to come in at the last minute and rescue the poor woman from her own ideas."

I tapped my finger on my chin. "I'll have to find some really good props."

"Too bad you don't know anyone who deals in flea market finds." Mom ate more of her fries. "They could help you find inexpensive décor or maybe tell you where you can rent some . . . It's good to have connections in business."

"Gage works for a prop warehouse," I said as I sipped my drink. "I wonder if they have anything I could use. Maybe something from one of the traveling Broadway productions."

"Speaking of plays, I wanted you to have lunch with me so that we can discuss the engagement party."

I frowned. "What does that have to do with plays?"

"Nothing." Mom waved her hand dismissively. "I needed to bring up the subject. It's called a segue."

"A bad segue," I muttered.

"The engagement party," she pressed. "I know you were worried we were rushing it. But if your sister is going to marry Warren, then I want to be able to tell everyone. Already your Aunt Betty is pressing me about the party."

"I have the venue, Mom. It's all under control. Seriously . . . Felicity and I even have the menu planned. I'm working with the W downtown. It's going to be great. I'm working on this *Great Gatsby* theme. Biplanes and Roaring Twenties to keep the plane theme going."

"Yes, Felicity told me." Mom picked at her fries.

"Okay, if you know, then what's up?"

"You're in good with the detective who is investigating the murder, aren't you? If you aren't, you should be."

"Yes, I know Detective Murphy," I said. "But you told me not to talk about the investigation."

"I told you not to rain on Felicity's choice. We are supporting her and Warren." Mom looked me in the eye. "But your father and I are worried about the investigation. We don't want to go through all this work and planning only to have something bad happen."

"Bad, like what?" I raised my right eyebrow. My sunglasses teetered on my nose.

"Felicity won't tell me anything about what the police are saying when it comes to Warren." Mom leaned forward. "Is he a serious suspect?"

"I certainly hope not," I said.

"But do you know if he is or if he isn't? Because I can't stand the fact that my baby was questioned and then I have to wait for an arrest. If we have this party and then they arrest Warren . . . oh, my, what it will do to your sister."

I patted my mother's hand to try to calm the distress I saw on her face. "Don't worry, Mom. I'm doing my best to stay in the loop on this thing. I didn't tell you because you made it clear you didn't want to know."

"I've changed my mind. I'm a grown woman. I can handle it. That said, I don't want you putting Warren down. I'm certain he didn't do anything bad."

"I agree, Mom," I said. "I'm certain Warren didn't do it, either."

"Good. So the detective, is he telling you anything? Should I be concerned that the police will do something silly and charge Warren?"

"Detective Murphy won't tell me anything." I shook my head and frowned. "I've been to see him twice in hopes he could keep me up-to-date on the investigation. But he refuses to do anything other than question me about what I saw."

"But you are a witness. You were there. You found the body. Surely he'd tell you the minute he figures out who did it . . ."

"I'm working on him, Mom." I patted some more. "I promise. I think Detective Murphy still considers me a suspect. So I have to be careful how I push him."

"*What?* That's ridiculous. You didn't even know the victim. Did you?"

"No, I didn't." I shook my head. "But I made the mistake of not figuring out he was dead and calling the cops the minute I discovered him in the bathroom. Detective Murphy thinks I'm covering up for someone."

"Who?"

"Warren or Felicity, I suppose."

"Well, that's silly." Mom pulled her hand out from under mine and sipped her pop. "Of course my baby didn't do it, and neither did Warren. I won't let the police even hint that they did. Do you understand? It would ruin the party and the one and only chance my baby has for happiness."

I flashed Mom a closed-mouth smile. Felicity was always her baby. I was her older daughter and that was nice, but being the one older came with responsibilities. Those responsibilities included ensuring the younger one was always happy.

"I won't let that happen," I said.

"Promise me, Pepper," Mom said, her gaze serious. "Promise me that you won't let them ruin Felicity's happiness."

"I promise."

Chapter 16

I was still mulling over what to do with Keith Emry's proposal party when I found myself back at the Executive Airport.

"Hi, Pepper." Jimmy leaned over the guard-shack window. "Did you bring more cupcakes?"

"Cookies." I lifted the bakery box of cookies I'd gotten from a nearby grocery store. It never hurt to bribe the gatekeeper.

"Come on in." Jimmy raised the gate. I pulled in and parked my old car next to his small beat-up Nissan. He opened the back of the shack. "How've you been?"

"I'm well." I climbed out of the car and slung my purse over my shoulder. Handing him the box of cookies, I declined the offer to come inside the shack. "If you don't mind, I'd like to look around a bit."

"Oh, I don't know if I can do that. Jeb's getting real funny about security since Randy got offed." He took the cookies from me.

"I understand." I ran my fingers along the strap of my purse. "How about if you sign me in and I go talk to Jeb? That way he can tell me himself if it's okay if I look around."

Jimmy thought about that for a full thirty seconds. I caught him checking out the cookies through the clear window in the box.

"There are chocolate chip and peanut butter in there," I mentioned casually.

"Yeah, hey, okay, I'll sign you in. Let me get you a visitor badge." He turned and the shack door slammed behind him. I took the moment to assess my surroundings. There was a camera at the entrance of the airport. The fence around the airport was eight feet tall. There was a light post one hundred yards out on either side of the gate.

Behind me were the hangars with wide parking areas for private jets to taxi into. There were about twenty cars parked in groups of two or three. I put my hand over my eyes to shade them from the sunlight. At the far end was a control tower with a handful of radar arrays and blinking lights.

I hadn't thought about the air traffic controllers. There had to be at least one. I wondered who they were and if they knew the janitor.

The shack door opened. Jimmy had chocolate on the corner of his face. "Here's your badge. I signed you in as a visitor for Jeb."

"Great, thanks." I clipped the visitor badge to my sweater. "Where is his office?"

"He's in hangar one." Jimmy pointed to the first building. "It's like the hangar you were in the other night. Jeb's office is the first one across from the restrooms."

"Got it." I glanced at the hangar. It wasn't likely I'd run into too many people between me and Jeb, but rules were rules. If I wanted to keep Jimmy's goodwill, then I needed to see Jeb first. Hopefully he would be just as cooperative.

"I'll let him know you're coming." Jimmy popped back into the shack and let the door slam behind him.

I squared my shoulders and headed toward hangar one. Jeb wasn't the nicest person in the world. I also wasn't sure what he thought of me as we had really never talked, but that didn't mean I couldn't use my charm and wit to get more information out of him.

The large hangar doors were closed, so I went in through the small metal door. Inside was quiet as a tomb and smelled of oil, jet fuel, and dust. The overhead lights buzzed. There was a single airplane on the far side of the hangar. Lights burned in the office area.

I lifted my chin, pasted on my best smile, and moved forward. "Hello?" I knocked on the open office door. "Mr. Donaldson?"

Jeb looked up from his papers. He had a scowl on his

face. His hair was cut even shorter than before, sort of like a Marine's. I think my dad called them high-and-tight cuts—not that Dad had to worry. He'd been bald most of my life.

Jeb's eyes were haunted and tired. "Oh, it's you."

"Jimmy said I should check with you about coming in and looking around."

He stood. His clothes were clean and pressed. I remembered what a big man Jeb was. His security uniform skimmed over solid biceps and well-muscled shoulders. The man clearly worked out. "Have a seat."

I sat in one of the two plastic chairs in front of his desk. "How are things?" I let my concern show in my tone of voice.

He sat down and ran his hand over his face. "This damn investigation has been bad for business." His brown gaze held a hint of vulnerability and worry.

"You look like you haven't slept."

"Why are you here, Miss Pomeroy?" His tone was sharp and suspicious.

"I want to know about Randy Stromer." I clutched my purse. "I feel sort of responsible for him." Jeb narrowed his eyes. I raised my hand in a stop motion. "I didn't kill him, I swear. I'd never seen a dead body before. Heck, I didn't even realize he was dead. And the police aren't telling me anything. I can't sleep, either. I want to know more about him. I want to know why someone would want to kill him."

"Randy was a good guy with a problem," Jeb said.

"Everyone here knew he had a problem. The only thing I can figure is that he pushed someone too hard or he owed the wrong people money. This is Chicago. Bookies tend to have mob connections."

"You think it was a mob hit?" I hadn't thought about mob connections or bookies or anyone like that. I mean, I watched movies and television. I knew these things sometimes happened, but this is the twenty-first century. Surely if it had been a professional hit, they would not have stuffed him into a stall in the ladies' room. "You know they're investigating Warren Evans, right? I mean, this is my sister's fiancé we're talking about. You don't think he did it, do you?"

"Mr. Evans seems like an okay guy. I don't see him doing that unless Randy attacked him, and then, I doubt he would have left him in the women's bathroom." Jeb frowned, deepening the lines in his face.

"What do you know about Laura Snow?" I asked. "I assume she's here all the time and you know her, right?"

"Laura?" Jeb leaned back. "Actually she isn't here all the time. She works part-time for Mr. Evans's company. When the economy went south, she picked up the flight attendant job. Otherwise, she works full-time at Shady Tree Manor. It's a nursing home for the elderly."

"That's an odd combination of careers," I said, surprised.

"Not really. She's a certified EMT. That works for both being a flight attendant and the nursing home."

"I hadn't thought about flight attendants being EMTs.

I suppose it kind of makes sense. They are trained for emergencies."

"It's their true job—ensuring passenger safety. Don't let the uniforms fool you. Those people are skilled. My daughter is a flight attendant out of O'Hare."

"Wow, you must be proud," I said.

"I am." Jeb nodded.

"What about Daniel Frasier?" I asked. "Did he know Randy?"

"Everyone knew Randy," Jeb acknowledged. "Daniel and Randy used to bet against each other. I think they knew the same bookie at one point, but then Daniel got married and straightened up his act. I don't think those two had done anything together for years."

Well, this was getting me nowhere. Unless Laura had access to drugs when she worked at the nursing home, but there didn't seem to be a motive for her to kill Randy. I sincerely doubted Laura was a mob hit man.

"What about the mechanics?" I asked. "There are mechanics that work on the airplanes, right?"

"Yes, the crew does preventative maintenance on each aircraft before it flies again. It's a thing with Mr. Evans's company. He says he wants to have a perfect record, and the only way to do that is to ensure a good ground crew and the best pilots." Jeb looked at his papers. "It costs extra, but that usually evens out with the number of requests for planes. Randy's death has hurt our reputation. I may have to lay off some of our top mechanics." He blew out a long breath. "In this economy, there isn't anywhere local they can go, and if they move to another state, who's going to buy their homes? Not with the glut of foreclosures on the market."

"I can see why you're worried." I leaned forward. "It sounds as if the sooner we can get this murder figured out, the better—for my sister and for your crew."

"I'm not an investigator." Jeb frowned. "I have work here." He waved over his stack of papers. "Besides, the cops want me to stay out of it. Didn't they tell you to stay out of it?"

"Yes, but as I said, this concerns my sister and her future happiness. Listen, I get it if you don't want to investigate. Let me see what I can do," I said. "Give me access to the grounds and the crew and I'll keep you in the loop."

"What about Detective Murphy?" Jeb asked.

"He won't share anything about the investigation." I shook my head. "But as far as I can tell, they are only looking at Warren and I really don't think he did it."

Jeb narrowed his eyes thoughtfully and let silence surround us. I let him figure out what he was going to do. I had made my case. Now it was up to him to give me permission or not.

"I suppose you're going to investigate whether I allow you to or not."

"Yes." I was honest. "I'd rather enter with a visitor badge on than have to figure out how to sneak past Jimmy."

Jeb gave me a thoughtful look. "I suppose it would be in my best interest to keep track of when you come and go."

"Does this mean you'll let me investigate?" I felt my spirits perk up.

"It means I'll let you on the property as long as you promise to always sign in with Jimmy and notify me immediately if you discover anything relevant to the case. That means no more sneaking around bribing my guys with cupcakes. Is that clear?"

I cringed. So he knew about the cupcakes. He'd probably hear about the cookies, as well. I might as well admit to it up front. I needed Jeb to trust me. "It's crystal clear," I agreed. "I won't sneak onto the property and I will let you know everything I know as soon as I know it."

"Good girl," he said. "The flight crew is out for today. Come back tomorrow around ten. I'll let Scott—our crew chief—know you're coming."

I stood. "Thank you, Jeb. This means a lot to me."

"If you can solve this thing quick, it will mean a lot to me as well. Now get out of here. I have work to do."

"Right." I left the office with a smile on my face. I'd just been given permission to conduct my own investigation into Randy's murder. There might be something helpful that I could learn. I mean, people would be more prone to tell me things that they wouldn't tell the cops. After all, I didn't have the ability to arrest them.

I hitched my purse over my shoulder and left hangar one. The first thing I was going to do was get the lay of the land. That meant walking around all the hangars and looking for entrances and exits. Taking pictures with my camera phone so that I could create a murder board, like the cops on television had.

Maybe, just maybe, I'd get lucky and find the killer before they struck again. Or before my baby sister's fiancé was arrested.

Chapter 17

My cell phone rang as I was walking about the airport. "Hello?"

"Hi, Pepper, this is Cesar."

"Hi," I said and put him on speaker so I could take pictures of hangar four with my phone. I tried not to think about how creepy it was to come back to the crime scene armed with nothing but my phone.

"I wanted to let you know I have the video done from your sister's engagement."

"Oh, awesome. That was fast."

"I did some editing and added music and ended with that picture montage you asked for along with their favorite song."

"Oh, she's going to love it!" I gushed in anticipation of Felicity's excitement.

"I've got the master stored on my server, but I've burned you a DVD. Let me know if you want more than one. I'll burn more for twenty dollars a pop."

"Great. I know Mom and Dad will want one and I want an extra as well. I'm building a portfolio. I've started my own business planning proposals and engagement parties."

"Wow, well, remember me if you want more video. I take a lot of footage then cut it down to the very best shots and put it together seamlessly."

"Send me your price list and I'll add it to my options."

"Cool."

I went to hang up when it occurred to me that he said he had a lot of footage. "Wait . . ."

"Yes?"

"Do you still have the raw footage of that night?"

"Sure, you never know when a client might want something switched out or added. Why?"

"No reason." I chewed on the inside of my mouth. "Do you mind if I see the raw footage?"

"Sure, I'll burn it to a separate DVD. Do you mind sharing your reason? It's a lot of film to watch just for fun."

"Why don't you bring both DVDs by my apartment later this evening and I'll explain."

"Will do." Cesar hung up. I took a couple more shots

of the empty hangar. It was locked up with yellow crime-scene tape across the door so there was no way I was going to get inside. But at the very least I had all four sides of the building. I could see the doors and the alleyways.

Maybe the pictures would stir some memory in Cesar. Maybe he caught evidence in his raw footage. I was surprised Detective Murphy hadn't asked to see it yet. I went back to my car, unlocked it, and waved to Jimmy, who waved back. I started old blue up and she hummed like only an old car can. There was something comforting about sitting in a big Oldsmobile boat. If I were ever attacked, I knew old blue would be solid metal between me and a killer.

All in all, it was a good day. Mom behaved herself at lunch for the most part. Jeb Donaldson was receptive to my wanting to investigate, and Cesar was willing to let me see his raw footage.

Everything was coming up roses until I saw the police lights in my rearview mirror. I checked my speed. Okay, so I was six miles per hour over the limit. I thought that was usually okay. I pulled to the side of the road. Maybe he simply wanted me to get over so he could go on by.

Yeah, that didn't happen. He pulled in behind me and parked. There is nothing more embarrassing than sitting on the side of the road with a cop car behind you. The flashing lights caught everyone's eye. When you got pulled over, passersby had to slow down and look to see what criminal had been caught in the act. I slumped deeper into old blue.

My heart pounded in my throat and my face was hot

from embarrassment. I remembered he'd probably want to see my license and registration. So I grabbed my purse and dug out my driver's license. I glanced at the awful photo. Why is it that you always look drunk in your driver's license photo? Did they do that on purpose?

A glance in the mirror told me the policeman had gotten out of his car and was headed toward my car. I opened my glove compartment and pulled out the book with my registration in it. Then I rolled down my window.

"Hello, Officer." I smiled brightly.

"Miss." He glanced in the car. "May I see your license and registration?"

"Sure, I have them right here." I handed him the two pieces of paper. "What's this all about?"

He glanced at them then slipped them onto the clipboard he carried. "I saw that you came out of the Executive Airport."

"Yes." My heart pounded in my chest. I tried to put on my most innocent expression.

"You realize that there was a murder there a few nights ago." He pinned me with his dark eyes. I could see them through his sunglasses.

"Yes, sir, I'm the one who found the body," I said and tried not to sound smug.

"Dispatch got a call from an employee telling us that they saw a suspicious woman taking pictures of the hangar where the murder happened." He tilted his head slightly and lowered his chin. "They gave the description of your car. Were you taking pictures of the hangar?"

"Yes," I said and folded my hands in my lap. "I didn't know that was a crime. Besides, I had permission from the head of security, Jeb Donaldson. You can call him and ask. Tell him it was Pepper Pomeroy who took the pictures."

"It's not a crime to take pictures," he said. "But it is suspicious. Have you heard of the saying, 'If you see something, say something'?"

"Yes."

He gave a short nod of his head. His eyes narrowed slightly. "Someone did."

"I see." I dropped my hands in my lap. "Like I said, I had permission from Jeb Donaldson, the head of airport security, to look around."

He glanced at my identification and then back at me. "Are you a reporter?"

"No."

"A private investigator?"

"Oh, gosh, no." I shook my head. "I'm an event planner. I planned Warren Evans's marriage proposal to my sister in a plane in that hangar. It's why I was there and why I found the body."

"I see. Had you been to the hangar prior to that day?"

"No." I frowned. "I told all of this to the officers who are investigating the murder. Call Detective Murphy. He'll tell you I'm cooperative."

"You do know that it is a crime to interfere with an investigation, right?"

"I wasn't interfering," I said. "I was merely taking pictures."

"I'll be right back." He walked back to his vehicle and climbed inside. I could see in my rearview mirror that he was checking my identification on his computer. Thank goodness I didn't have any outstanding parking tickets and my plates were all current.

There really wasn't anything he could do. Was there? I glanced at the time on my phone. It was 6 P.M. Which meant rush hour traffic would be winding down. I still had some work to do at home if I hoped to get the invitations sent out for the engagement party. Plus Cesar was scheduled to come by with the engagement video. Then there was Keith's event to put together, and I wanted to call Michael today to find out if he was interested in my services and see how he would feel about my fees. I planned to have to negotiate some of the fees, but would stick firm on others. Keith said that Michael had money, so I made a silent promise that I would not undervalue myself or my abilities.

It's what I had done for so long with Bobby. I had undervalued my love and my worth as a woman and a partner. All out of fear that I wouldn't find anyone else who would see past my frizzy red hair to the heart underneath.

Silly, I suppose. But truly, I deserved a man like Warren. One who went out of his way to try to please me. Someone who would plan a romantic proposal and know me so well he would have the ring of my dreams already sized and ready to slip on my finger.

What was so wrong with wanting a man who wanted you more than beer, more than pool, more than countless nights at a bar?

Warren showed me there were men out there who were different. Now all I had to do was figure out how to find one.

The police officer slammed his car door and came back to my window with a clipboard in hand. He wrote a note on it. "Your right taillight is out."

"Oh, I didn't know."

He ripped a pink sheet off the clipboard. "It's a fifty-dollar fine. I'd recommend you replace both taillights at the same time so that it doesn't happen again."

"Yes, sir," I said and took the ticket along with my ID and registration.

He leaned down into my window. "Let me give you another piece of advice."

"Okay." I drew my eyebrows together. He made me nervous with his cool cop gaze.

"Stay away from the murder scene. Too many murderers get involved in investigations. You don't want to throw suspicion on yourself, now do you?"

"No, sir." I shook my head. "I simply want to keep the suspicion off Warren Evans. He's going to marry my sister."

"Detective Murphy is the best," the officer said. "He'll catch the guy who did this—even if that person is Warren

Evans. Your involvement will not stop him from finding the killer."

"I was only trying to help . . ." I looked up with my most innocent expression.

"The best way to help is to let the professionals do their job. Have I made myself clear?"

"Yes," I said and held back a sigh.

"Good." He tugged on the bill of his hat. "Take care of yourself and your car."

"Okay." I watched him walk back to his car. Then I rolled up my window and put my paperwork away. Sheesh, a fifty-dollar fine all because my back taillight went out. I knew I wouldn't have gotten a ticket if someone at the airport hadn't called me out as suspicious. I had to wonder . . . were they really worried about my taking pictures or had I made someone nervous that I might learn something they didn't want anyone to know about?

This brought me back to Cesar and the raw footage of that day. Maybe, just maybe, he caught something important. Whoever called the cops on me wouldn't know that. Which meant I didn't have to go back to the airport to continue my investigation. Unless, of course, there was something left to investigate. But then I'd take Jimmy or Jeb with me and I'd make darn sure my car was working properly.

Chapter 18

My day went from bad to worse.

"Bobby, what are you doing here?" I asked as I came up the steps to find him hanging out in the hallway next to my apartment.

"You put my stuff out in the hall." His tone was accusatory. He shoved his hands in his pockets. "I proposed marriage and you put my stuff out in the hall. What is going on with you, Pepper?"

I clutched my keys in my hand. "Come on, Bobby, you didn't really mean that proposal."

"What if I did?" He shrugged. His leather jacket, plaid shirt, and jeans looked like they needed a good cleaning. His hair was shaggy, and for the first time I noticed the paunch around his stomach and the softness in his jaw.

"A man who means to propose does not complain about getting down on one knee and does not sneer his proposal as if it were the dumbest idea in the world. He also doesn't start by saying, 'I suppose you want to get married now . . .'"

"Hey, baby, look, if I had known you wanted hearts and flowers, I would have given them to you. You know that."

"No, I don't know that." I pushed him aside to unlock my door. "If you really loved me, you would know better than to give me some lame proposal." I turned and faced him. "Face it. Bobby, we've been over for a long time. We've only been going through the motions because it was easy."

He narrowed his eyes. "Trust me, baby, there isn't anything about you that's easy."

I winced. The man knew how to hurt me. "Then you must be relieved to be done with me." I shoved my key in the lock. "Now you don't have to work so hard." I slipped inside and went to shut my door in his face, but Bobby was stronger than me. He held the door open.

"Come on, baby," he said. "Don't do this. Look, I'll be better. I'll even get you that ring you've been eyeing at Pond's Jewelry Store."

"What ring?" I was confused.

"The one with the square diamond and the blue stones."

I searched my memory. "Bobby, I haven't been in Pond's Jewelry Store in four years."

"See, I remember what you like." He looked pleased with himself.

"No, Bobby, you don't." I sighed. "You and I never looked at rings together. In fact, I don't remember ever going to Pond's with you." I frowned. "Who did you go to Pond's with?"

Guilt washed over his face. "You, baby," he said. "You're the only one for me."

"It was Cindy Anderson, wasn't it?" I pursed my lips.

The look on his face was priceless . . . at once guilty and smug.

Cindy Anderson was two years behind us in school. She was blond and worked as a barista at Starbucks. She'd been sniffing around Bobby for the last two years. I had suspected he liked it. I never thought he'd actually acted on it.

"Good-bye, Bobby." I closed the door in his face. This time he let me. I threw the dead bolt into place and went to the kitchen. My hands shook as I set down my keys and purse. Bobby had been two-timing me and had even gone ring shopping. When was he going to tell me? After he got married?

I leaned against the sink and tried to calm my upset stomach. Did he think he could have us both? Then I realized that he probably did believe that. After all, he'd already been doing it for a while.

I took off my coat and hung it up in the closet. Then I poured myself a glass of wine and sat down on my couch. For a smart woman, I sure hadn't realized how bad my relationship had gotten. The room seemed so bare with his things gone.

"Room for new things in my life," I said aloud and raised my wineglass. New things from my list, and all purchased with Warren's seed money. They sat in boxes along the wall that once held Bobby's game collection.

"No sense in crying over how stupid I've been." I rolled up my sleeves and distracted myself from Bobby by ripping open boxes and reading instructions. The desk and chair had to be put together. The computer and printer and fax had to be connected.

Four hours later, my new business was set up in my ex–living room. I cleared away the boxes of Chinese take-out that I'd ordered halfway through figuring out how to put the desk together. I wiped everything off with a dust cloth and carefully arranged my business cards and calendar.

My apartment was small, but without Bobby in my life, there really was no need for a living room. I moved my TV and DVD player into my tiny bedroom. The rest of my stuff was put in the kitchen.

I arranged the love seat–sized couch to face my desk, which was angled in the corner. That way clients could have a comfortable place to sit. The tiny table that I used to use for my dining room table was now set up with a display of local venues and photos of some of the events I had planned in my old job. There was a poster board set up on an easel with all the pieces of Felicity's proposal event and then the pieces of her upcoming engagement party.

There was a second poster board on an easel with Keith's proposal written across the top. So far I had brainstormed a mermaid theme. There were two possible venues in mind—one was Shedd Aquarium and the other was the large inside-outside heated pool at a resort in Saint Charles.

I had calls in to both venues for pricing and availability. Once the venue was set, I would need decorations. I smiled, remembering once again that Gage worked at a prop warehouse. I glanced at my watch. It was after midnight.

Cesar must have gotten busy. He hadn't stopped by with the DVDs. I shrugged. If he didn't show in the next day or two, I'd call him and remind him. As for now, it was time to go to bed. In the morning I would call Gage and see what he had that I could rent or purchase. Maybe he'd have a treasure chest. I could match the things that the Little Mermaid collected in the chest along with sparkly baubles to please Amy.

It was going to be an amazing proposal event.

* * *

The next morning I called Gage.

"Trinity Prop House, this is Gage speaking, how can I help you?"

"Hi, Gage, it's Pepper. How are you?"

"Pepper, great to hear from you. How've you been?"

I turned my new office chair to the window to watch the Metra train rattle by. "I'm good actually. No, no, I'm great."

"That's good to hear. I was a bit worried about you after the last time I saw you."

I cringed. "I'm sorry you had to see that," I said.

"Yeah, I don't know what Bobby was thinking."

"He wasn't," I said. "It doesn't matter. All in all, it was a huge wake-up call for me." I sighed. "After seeing how happy Felicity is and how much Warren cherishes her, I realized that Bobby and I were still stuck in a high school relationship. You know, where he was the cool football guy and I was happy for any attention he gave me." I cringed at my own description. Until that moment I hadn't realized how true it was. I swallowed. "Not cool."

"Bobby's still trying to relive high school," Gage said quietly. "Seriously, I'm glad you broke it off."

"Me, too," I said and took a deep breath. "I packed up all his stuff and put it in the hallway. I had no idea how much he had taken over my life. The worst thing was I let him."

"So you are really okay with it being over?" Gage asked.

"More than okay," I said and realized the relief I felt was real. "I'm ready for a new start. I didn't tell you, but Warren not only paid me for planning the proposal, but he suggested I go into business for myself as a proposal planner."

"A proposal planner? That sounds interesting. Tell me about it."

I always liked how Gage took the time to find out what I was doing. It was so refreshing compared to Bobby. It's why Gage and I were good friends. "I came up with a business plan. Remember how Professor Gideon made me do one for my degree? Well, I copied that and put together this whole idea. Then I gave the plan to Warren and he agreed to be my silent partner."

"Wow, that's amazing. Warren sounds like a great guy."

"He is," I said. "Felicity is happy."

"Good for her."

"Listen, Warren gave me the name of his buddy Keith, who was having trouble coming up with a romantic proposal and Keith agreed to let me plan it and put it in my portfolio."

"Nice."

"Right?" I turned back to my computer and wiggled my mouse to bring up my ideas. "Anyway I'm doing this proposal on the house, and Keith is going to let me use it in my brochures and website as an example."

"Cool."

"Which brings me to you. I was wondering if I could rent some stuff from the prop house. I'm doing this first one on a very limited budget since I'm not getting paid. Would it be weird for you to help out? I mean, I know you and Bobby are friends and I don't want to jeopardize that, but . . ."

"Hey, sure, anything for you, Pepper. In fact, why don't you come down and we can pull out some items—free of charge."

"Oh." Amazement at his generosity rushed through me. "That would be fabulous. I'll be sure and let everyone know where I got the props. In fact, give me some of your business cards and I'll send people your way."

"That would be great," Gage said. "When is a good time to meet?"

"How about tomorrow?" I said. "At two?"

"That works," Gage said. "It will be good to see you."

"It will be good to see you, too. Who knows? I may be helping you plan your proposal soon—no charge."

There was a strange silence on the other end of the line. I never was good at awkward silences. "So I'll see you tomorrow?"

"Okay." Gage hung up the phone.

I frowned and looked at my phone as if it could tell me what I had done wrong. Then I shrugged. Maybe Gage and his girl were having problems. He never was much for talking about his girlfriends. I figured it was a guy thing.

Now, to call the venues and see which one was willing to work with me. It was the venue that would determine the props I needed. If I was going to pick out props tomorrow, I needed to have a venue today. There was no time to waste!

Chapter 19

I had no idea how dull watching video without music and narration could be. Yawning, I resisted the urge to fast-forward through the DVD.

Cesar had brought the raw footage by my apartment that afternoon. The DVD of the proposal was great. He'd added music and had Warren narrate. Felicity's face shone with surprise and tears, and the romance of the entire thing had me sighing.

In fact, the video was so good I asked Cesar if I could add it to my portfolio. I had him leave me several business cards for clients as well. Even if they didn't use my services, I didn't mind promoting Cesar's business. He had done such a great job.

I sat cross-legged on my bed in my purple and white

polka-dotted flannel pajamas. The pants were baggy and comfy. The shirt was warm and buttoned down the front. Bobby had hated the set, but I always loved how soft and warm they were.

There was a plate of cheese and crackers and a bowl of tortilla chips next to me. I won't mention the peanut M&M's or the glass of wine that was half full on my nightstand. Yes, I was in full-on single-girl mode. The worst part was the crumbs in the bed. I shrugged the thought off and grabbed a triangle-shaped chip and shoved it in my mouth.

At least snack crumbs could be easily brushed away and swept up in the morning. My apartment might be small and old but it had hardwood floors. These crumbs were the hard-won crumbs of single life. It was the first time I'd eaten in bed since high school. Mom never let me eat snacks in my bedroom and then I'd been dating Bobby. I'd kept the room spotless on the off chance things got romantic.

Crumbs on a single girl's bed were one thing. Crumbs in a bed with a guy were just tacky. At the moment I didn't mind that I was four cats away from being a crazy cat lady. I snatched another chip and reached for my wine when something in the video caught my eye.

"What was that?" I grabbed my remote, knocking over the bowl of chips and leaning into the plate, crushing the crackers. I pressed stop and the thirty-second rewind. Mesmerized by the video, I pressed play. There it was. The clue I'd been waiting for.

Cesar had the camera on his shoulder and came down the stairs to give the viewer a shot of the plane. As he came around the front, I spotted Laura Snow in the danger zone of the plane behind the jet engines. Then I saw her opening the "authorized personnel only" door that Daniel Frasier had warned me to stay away from. That wasn't what caught my eye. I mean, as far as I knew, Laura was authorized personnel. What caught my eye was the fact that she was clearly talking to someone.

She had her left hand on her hip and gestured with her right. Someone else was inside the door. There! Was that blob a hand that waved toward her? I stopped the video and looked at it again. It was only a glimpse and hard to tell if it was a man's hand or a woman's hand, but clearly someone was there. It appeared that Laura was arguing with them and they were arguing back.

Ha! I leapt out of bed, cracker crumbs tumbling about as I went closer to the screen. I paused the DVD, but even nose to television, I couldn't tell who it was Laura argued with. Then in the next frame she must have heard a noise because she looked straight at the camera. Her eyebrows were drawn down. Her mouth tightened and her eyes flashed.

The next frame blurred to the cockpit as if Cesar had turned around quickly. Inside was Daniel—he waved to the camera and smiled. Cesar continued on to take video of the rest of the hangar. Then he scooted inside the plane and hid in the bathroom, waiting for Felicity and Warren to come in.

My heart pounded in my chest and I did a little bare-foot dance in the crumbs. There was someone else on the scene. That meant we had proof that it wasn't Warren who killed the janitor. The best part was I could mail the invitations to the engagement party and we could move forward as soon as I showed the tape to Detective Murphy.

I grabbed a broom and swept up the mess of crumbs. Then I marked the time on the DVD. Taking one final look at the video frame with the blur that was clearly someone's hand, I wondered if the crime scene techs could tell me if it was a male hand or a female hand. If it was female, Warren would really be off the hook. Oh—wait—a female hand might implicate me. I winced at the thought. I was the only other known female at the hangar. I studied the hand and glanced at my own. It didn't take an expert to see that I was not the person on the tape. The size and shape were nowhere near the same. That got me off the hook.

I went to sleep that night safe in the thought that I'd not only saved my sister's engagement party, but saved her entire future. She would no longer live with the fear that Warren could be arrested any day and charged with murder. All because he was in a hangar to give her the plane proposal of her dreams.

* * *

I was up at the crack of dawn. My excitement and triumph had me dressing in jeans and a long-sleeved T-shirt in record time. The blue tee matched my eyes. I brushed my hair and twisted it into a messy bun. Gathered up the DVD and my handbag and keys and off I went.

Detective Murphy didn't get in to his office until 9 A.M.

"Why are you back here, Ms. Pomeroy?"

I followed Detective Murphy from the front door to his desk and then to the police-issue coffeepot. He poured his cup full of the strong black brew and then opened ten packs of sugar.

"I have proof that Warren Evans didn't kill the janitor," I said. It was hard to keep my excitement out of my voice.

"Pepper." He turned to me. His hound dog jaw shook and his thick right eyebrow rose. "What are you talking about?"

I followed him back to his desk. "I have my videographer's raw footage right here." I waved a copy of the disc. "Do you have a DVD player?"

"We do." He sat down. He was so calm—almost too calm—as he eyed me and my DVD.

"Can I show you what I found?" I thought he would be more excited. I was so excited I fairly shook with energy.

"You can leave the tape here. I'll have our team go over it."

"But I want to show you." My voice rose an octave. "It's proof that someone else was there. Someone Laura Snow was talking to. In fact, it looked as if she argued with them. I think it's the killer."

"Are you sure it wasn't the janitor?"

"No, I don't think so. It was hard to tell. You see, they

were behind the authorized-personnel door. The one on the back of the plane—the opening that Daniel told me about."

"Authorized-personnel door . . ." he repeated as if he had never heard of such a thing.

"You know, the door behind the engines to the back. Daniel—the pilot . . ."

"I know who Daniel is," Detective Murphy interjected as he stirred his coffee.

"Daniel told me that it was off-limits and for authorized personnel only."

"And was Miss Snow authorized?"

"I imagine." I shrugged. "But it still means she could have been arguing with the killer."

"Does the film show where the others in the hangar were?"

"It pans to Daniel in the cockpit."

"Anyone else?"

I wrinkled up my nose and narrowed my eyes. "No, but I know that wasn't Warren arguing with Laura Snow."

"I thought you said you could only see a glimpse of whomever she talked to—"

"Argued with," I corrected. "I'm telling you she looks mad in the video. Her hands are waving about, and the tone of her voice is thick with anger."

"Can you hear what she's saying?"

"Well, no . . . but wait until you see her face."

"Fine, let's say she did argue with someone outside by the back of the plane. It doesn't prove anything."

"Right, but don't you see, there was no way it could have been Warren. Really just a few minutes later Cesar is in the bathroom and the video—"

"Wait, Cesar was in the bathroom? The one with the dead body?"

I shook my head. "No, the bathroom on the plane. We put him in there to secretly record the proposal."

"There was a guy in a private jet bathroom taping the main cabin." He turned his head and looked at me out of the narrowed corner of his eye. "I think there are laws against that . . ."

"It's fine." I blew out a long breath. "Warren knew he was being taped. In fact, everyone knew but Felicity, and she has no problem with the moment being recorded. In fact, she is thrilled with it."

"Hmmm." He took a long slurp of his coffee.

"I'm trying to tell you that this recording is proof Warren didn't kill the janitor." I waved the disc at him. "There was someone else in the authorized-personnel-only part of the plane."

"It proves nothing," Detective Murphy said. "Only that at some point someone was in the back of the plane stowing things for the trip. You yourself said that you can't see who the person is."

I placed the disc on his desk and pursed my mouth. "You could ask Laura Snow. It's a line of inquiry I know you haven't checked because you didn't know about it. Now you do." I waved at the DVD. "Check it."

Detective Murphy sipped his coffee and wiggled his computer mouse. The action brought up whatever report he had on his computer.

I waited in silence for him to say something. It was hard. I'm not good at long silences. But this time I was going to stick around until I was heard, and if that meant I had to stay in my seat and wait for Detective Murphy, then I would wait.

After what seemed like an hour, but a quick glance at the clock told me was only three minutes, he looked up. "You're still here?"

"Of course I'm here." I clutched the strap of my handbag.

He looked at me square on and I looked back. Finally he nodded once. "Fine. I'll look at it."

"Thank you!" I didn't even try to keep the perturbed tone out of my voice. "Should I put it in the DVD player?"

"Later."

"Oh." My shoulders fell and my heart sank.

"You can go, Pepper."

"You will look at it, right?" I eyed the DVD as I rose.

"I will look at it." He raised an eyebrow at me. "I don't lie."

That look was clearly accusatory. "I didn't lie, either," I said. "I really didn't know he was dead."

"Have a good day, Ms. Pomeroy." He waved his hand and pointed his head toward the door.

"Right." It was tough to leave. I mean, how would I

know if he even looked at the tape? How would I know that he would try to find out who was inside the plane? And why was Laura arguing with them?

"Are you sure . . ."

"Have a good day, Pepper," he said.

"But—"

"You have to trust me to do my job. I trust that you will spend the day doing yours."

Ugh. He was right. I left the police station. I had venues to check on and a contract to sign. At least for today I would have to take Detective Murphy at his word.

Chapter 20

ॐ

"Pepper, they arrested Warren!" Felicity's horrified voice came through my cell phone.

I sat up in bed and ran my hand over my face. A glance at the clock told me it was 9 A.M. I had been up until two working out the details for the sunken treasure proposal. My appointment with Gage wasn't until 11 A.M., and I had set my alarm for 9:30 A.M. in hopes of getting at least seven hours of sleep.

"What?" I pushed my black and white sleep mask up into my hair like a headband. I shoved my new pink-flowered comforter off me and swung my legs around.

"Warren, it's on the news. Oh, Pepper! How could they do this?" Felicity's wail could have been heard the next block over.

My fuzzy mind worked hard to put the pieces together. I picked up the remote and turned on my television. "They would not arrest Warren." I got out of bed. "I talked to Detective Murphy yesterday. He didn't mention a thing about bringing Warren in. In fact, we talked about the possibility of a third person on the scene."

"It's on the news!" Felicity stomped her foot. I could hear it hit the hardwood through the phone.

The commercial ended and a Breaking News headline was running across the screen: MILLIONAIRE ENTREPRENEUR, WARREN EVANS, ARRESTED FOR THE MURDER OF JANITOR AT THE COOK COUNTY EXECUTIVE AIRPORT.

"There must be some mistake," I said. "It's a typo or something."

"It's not a typo." Felicity's voice wavered. "It's Warren. They showed him being taken away with his hands cuffed behind his back. This is terrible. What should I do?"

"Calm down and breathe." I grabbed my bathrobe from the hook on the back of my bedroom door and walked across my cold wood floor in my bare feet. "Does Warren have a lawyer?"

"Yes."

"Call him."

"I'm pretty sure Warren would have done that already," Felicity said. "But I can check."

"Good, then send Warren a text asking if he needs you to do anything." A glance in the mirror startled me. My hair stood up on end, mimicking Einstein. A train rattled by and I could see the news clip playing on the television behind me. There was Detective Murphy talking to the press.

"Felicity," I said as a thought crossed my mind.

"Yes?"

"Where are you?"

"I'm at work. You know I work eight thirty A.M. to five P.M."

"Honey, you need to hang up and go see your boss. If the reporters are smart, they're going to want to interview you next. They will know you were with him that night."

"Oh!"

"Don't talk to anyone but your boss," I said. "Then only warn your boss that you think there will be reporters snooping around and tell her why."

"You mean that Warren was arrested—"

"Yes, and then stop talking. I know you love your coworkers but this is a big story and people would pay for the inside scoop."

"Oh, Pepper, my coworkers wouldn't really talk to reporters about me. Would they?"

"They will," I said as calmly as I could. "It's not personal. Some may even think they're helping you. You can't tell anyone anything." I picked up my brush and battled my hair back into a messy ponytail and grabbed a rubber band to secure it. "I'm getting dressed. I will be there to pick you up as soon as I can."

It would take me at least thirty minutes to get to her if I left at this very moment. One glance at my pajamas and I knew I had to take five minutes to get dressed. The last thing I wanted was to appear on camera in my rattiest pajamas. If the press caught sight of me taking Felicity home, they would try to take pictures. I needed to look professional. Who knew what possible future clients would be watching?

Felicity worked in downtown Chicago. "I'll text you when I get there and let you know whether you need to sneak out a back way or not."

"What? Why can't I wait out front for you?"

"Felicity, you might be mobbed by reporters. They're going to try to get you to talk any way they can. I'll be there to pick you up soon. Hang tight."

"Okay . . ." Her voice wavered. "Pepper, I know he didn't do it."

"So do I, honey, so do I." I hung up the phone and splashed water on my face.

Five minutes later I was dressed in black slacks, a black turtleneck sweater, dressy black shoes, and big dark sunglasses. I wanted to fit in downtown so that no one would suspect I had anything to do with Felicity. I grabbed my keys, locked my door, and rushed to my car.

Mrs. Horowicz, who lived in the apartment under mine, was in the parking lot. "Hello, Pepper."

"Hi, Mrs. H." I did not have time to stop and chat. But Mrs. H never took that as a reason not to chat me up, so I sped by her and stuck my key into old blue's driver-side door to unlock it. "Have a nice day."

I opened the door and climbed into the car. When I

reached for my door to close it, Mrs. Horowicz stood in the way. I found her odd, silent speed a little creepy.

"Was that your sister's fiancé they arrested this morning for murdering that poor janitor?" She held my door open with her hand and peered down at me.

"I'm sorry, what?" I tried to stall and pull my car door closed.

The old woman was having none of it. She clung to the door like her life depended on it. Mrs. H had lived in our apartment building her entire married life, some sixty years. Her husband had died ten years ago, or so she told me. She'd stayed because it was the only home she knew.

Mrs. H was all of five feet tall and nearly as wide as she was tall. Today she wore a big flowered bib apron over a pale blue track suit. Her gray hair was short and permed to within an inch of its life. She was one of those older women who still went to the salon once a week to get their hair done. Then if it was windy or damp, she wore a plastic rain cap tied neatly under her chin. She was always careful to take it off as soon as she went inside. I don't think I'd ever seen her without her short, permed hair.

"I've been watching Channel Five all morning and they said that a Warren Evans was arrested for murder. I could have sworn he was Felicity's fiancé."

"I didn't have the news on," I said. "I'm certain my mother would have called me if Felicity were in any sort of trouble." I sent her a bright smile. "I'm late for an appointment downtown. Did you hear if the traffic was bad?"

"They said it was running thirty minutes on the Kennedy all morning."

"Thanks." I yanked my door out of her grasp and closed it. A quick crank of my engine and I waved her back without opening my window. "Talk to you later."

I pulled out of my parking space and glanced in my rearview mirror to see her still standing there. Her mouth was pursed and to the side. Her eyes glowed fiercely. She clearly suspected me of lying, but that was the trick—I didn't lie. I simply didn't tell her what she wanted to hear.

* * *

Four hours later, Mom and I had sequestered Felicity in my aunt Betty's home in Itasca. Aunt Betty was my grandma's half sister and we hoped the press would not be able to track my sister there.

I left them all sitting around Aunt Betty's kitchen table sipping tea and making outrageous plans to rescue Warren. I did one better. I headed to the police station to see Detective Murphy.

"You can't go in there," the officer at the reception desk called after me as I pushed the door open and stormed back to Detective Murphy's desk. The officer scooted around the counter with his hand on his gun belt. "Seriously." He tried to catch me, but I was faster and lighter on my feet. "Don't make me have to arrest you."

"I'll only be a moment," I said. "Besides, I'm certain Detective Murphy is expecting me."

"He is," the officer confirmed. "I have specific orders not to let you come back here."

"Too late." I scrambled around the desks, avoiding his reaching hand. "Detective Murphy." I narrowed my eyes at the sight of the man. "How could you do this? I was in here yesterday showing you how there was someone else in the hangar."

I walked up to his desk with a head full of steam. The duty desk officer finally caught up and tried to grab my arm. "I wouldn't touch me if I were you." I raised an index finger at him.

"I'm sorry, Murphy," he said. "She's quicker than I thought."

"It's okay." The detective sat back in his chair. "I'll handle her." He waved the officer off.

I glared at him. "What do you mean by that?"

"Have a seat, Pepper." He waved toward the plastic chair I had occupied the day before.

"I will not." I put my hands on my hips. "Not until you tell me why you arrested Warren after I provided you with evidence that there was someone else in that airplane. Someone else who may have had a reason to kill Randy."

"Pepper, I'm doing my job—by the book, I might add." The detective's mouth tightened into a thin line. "Do you think I wanted to arrest Warren Evans? The man has already hired the best lawyers in town to defend him. With his kind of money, I had to have an iron-clad case."

"Well, there's a hole in your iron-clad case big enough to drive a truck through," I said.

"If that's true, I'm certain the offices of McMillian and McMillian will find it." He raised one bushy eyebrow.

"I'm going to give Warren and his lawyers a copy of that raw footage," I warned him.

"You do that, Pepper." He went back to the paperwork on his desk. "Now, I have a job to do. Let me suggest you attend to yours as well."

"Oh, you can be sure I will," I warned and stormed off. "This entire thing is a miscarriage of justice."

I kept picturing the tears in Felicity's blue eyes as she sat at Aunt Betty's kitchen table. There was no way I could let Detective Murphy make this horrible mistake. Besides, I liked the guy. Someone had to save him from himself.

Chapter 21

The next day I had to leave a distraught Felicity with Aunt Betty and Mom and Dad. We had all gotten very good at taking side roads and ensuring we weren't followed.

So far no reporters had shown up at Aunt Betty's house. I have no idea what we would do with Felicity if they found her hiding spot.

"Make sure she doesn't watch the news," I said on my way out of the house. "It will only distress her."

"No problem," Dad said. "Your mom picked up the entire season of *New Girl*. We'll keep her busy."

I frowned and chewed on my bottom lip. "I hate to have to go, but I have to set up for Keith's proposal. I invited Mike to attend. If he likes it, I'm going to bill him full price for his proposal."

"Go," my mom said as she came out of the back bedroom. "We're fine here."

"Thanks, Mom." I kissed her on the cheek and left. The resort was twenty minutes away, and set up for Keith's proposal was this morning. Everything had to be right for Keith or my fledgling business would never get off the ground.

I pulled into the parking lot and parked in the back near the indoor-outdoor pool. We had already had our first frost. So the warmth of the heated pool steamed in the autumn air. I cut through a courtyard and walked in a back door using the pass key card the event manager had given to me.

Gage stood in the hallway and watched the workmen through the giant glass partition that separated the pool area from the rest of the resort.

"Hi, Gage." I greeted him with a kiss on the cheek and a hug. He hugged me back. I'd forgotten how tall and solid he was. Gage wore dark jeans and a light blue collared shirt. His shirt had been expertly ironed, creating a crisp line across his shoulders. He smelled good, of faint aftershave and ironing starch. There was something about the scent of pressed dress shirt warmed by a man's skin that did it for me.

Maybe it was because the scent of ironing reminded me of sitting with my mom watching her do laundry. Or maybe it reminded me of my dad when he and Mom would go out for date night. Whatever it was, I loved the scent.

"Wow, Pepper, I can't believe you pulled this venue off in such a short time."

"I got lucky. A friend of mine knows the event manager and discovered that the pool area's event for today was canceled last minute. I was able to step in and reserve it for a quarter of its regular price."

Gage shook his head. "You are good."

"Thanks . . . and thanks for letting me rent the props." I waved toward the pool and the workmen who were installing everything. "Keith's girlfriend likes scuba diving and girly sparkly things, so I'm going with a *Little Mermaid* theme. See how they are setting up a sunken ship in the center?"

"Yes. That prop was used as a three-quarter replica for exterior shots in the movie *Pirates*."

"It fits perfectly in the pool, don't you think?" I eyed the replica ship. "Anyway, I've got these great plans going on." I pulled my design sheets out of my fake-alligator-skin tote. "See how we're setting up not only the ship but miniatures of various places. Outside will be the Arctic Circle."

"That sounds right." Gage laughed and pointed at the snow that fell in soft, fat flakes.

"I can't believe it's snowing." I shook my head. "Good thing I planned for snow. Inside the pool area, we have the mermaid station, the kraken station, and the conch station." I walked him over to three four-foot-by-three-foot wide boxes stacked in the foyer. "I've got a lot of baubles and things. They are going to get into scuba gear compliments of City-Scuba and then follow the clues step-by-step until they find this treasure chest."

I pulled a treasure box out. It was small, only ten inches wide and eight inches tall. I'd actually purchased it because I wanted Keith to give it to his girl as a keepsake.

"Is that real?" Gage looked at the box. His blue eyes shone with interest.

"Yes." I handed him the box. "It's a high-end jewelry box. See, the inside is lined with silk and velvet." I moved closer to Gage and opened the lid. "Keith will bring the engagement ring tonight in its box. I will nestle that box inside the treasure chest. The box is Tiffany blue. There is no way she'll know before the chest opens." I sighed at the romance of it all.

"Nice, but how do you plan on keeping the treasure chest dry?" He turned it over in his hands. "This looks like mahogany. Tough wood, but not exactly waterproof."

"Oh, no problem." I dug in my tote and pulled out two bags. "These were made specifically to be waterproof to a depth of five meters—more than adequate for this pool." The bag came in two parts. The first was a padded zip bag and the second was a black bag with a serious seal.

"And you thought of this?" His voice was soft and he sounded impressed. His eyes sparkled and his mouth lifted at the corners, causing the creases at the edges of his eyes to deepen.

"Yeah." I blushed. "It's a gift." I said that to defuse the attention and compliment.

"No, it's a talent." He handed me the chest. "You are amazing."

"Aw, so are you." I put the chest and the waterproof bags into the top box and set it aside. "It means so much that I can call you and rent out props like these." I waved toward the pool where the workmen set up the underwater stations.

Gage shoved his hands in his pockets. "I'm happy to help you, Pepper." We both watched the guys at work for a moment. "You know, Emma and I have broken up."

I glanced at him. "Really? I'm sorry to hear that."

"You are?" He drew his eyebrows together, and his mouth went into a straight line.

"Of course," I said, and then noticed that the hotel equipment manager, Bill Pope, was heading toward us.

"Hey, Ms. Pomeroy," Bill said. "What did you want done with the stuff in these boxes?" He waved to the boxes. "They came in last night and I wasn't sure how they fit in with the plans you drew up."

"Oh, sure, grab a box and I'll show you where this stuff goes."

I bent to pick up a box when Bill put his hand out. "Let the guys get that." He waved over a porter. "Take this into the pool area." He turned to me. "Union rules."

"Of course," I said. I didn't mind. It was nice to let the men do the heavy lifting. Bobby usually left me to do that. "I'll follow you in." I stopped and glanced at Gage, who appeared to be upset. I put my hand on his arm.

"Hey, it's okay. Maybe we could get together and talk about Emma later."

"Right." His tone was tight. His shoulders shrugged. "I'll see you later."

"Okay, bye, Gage." I kissed his cheek and turned to Bill. "Now, I'll show you how cool these props are when you add them to the stations."

Somewhere in the back of my mind, I knew Gage had stormed off. I figured he was really upset about Emma. I made a mental note to set up a time to talk to him about how to win her back. Right now, I was a half an hour from seeing Keith and showing him what I'd set up.

I was so excited that I could barely wait. A glance at my watch told me Cesar would be here in two hours. Everything had to be picture perfect by then.

* * *

"I want to hear all about it," Felicity said.

It was my turn to stay with her at Aunt Betty's house. She and I were in our pajamas in the back bedroom. There were two twin beds in the bedroom with a nightstand between them. It always reminded me of the old, original *I Love Lucy* show with Lucy and Ricky sleeping in twin beds.

"It was perfect," I said with a sigh. "She thought she was there to shoot a kids' show on scuba diving. You know, something like swimming is fun, not scary."

"But she wasn't." Felicity's eyes sparkled.

"She wasn't. Her entire family was sequestered in a nearby ballroom. Cesar was there shooting video."

"How did you hide him this time?"

"Oh, I didn't." I shook the nail polish I had brought to do a pedicure. It was called "We Know Ya Wanna" and was a brilliant aqua blue. "Cesar did some great shots beforehand. Did you know they make underwater camera gear?"

Felicity nodded. "Yes, silly, it's how they do those diving documentaries."

"Right." I rolled up my plaid pajama pants to expose my ankles. "Anyway, Cesar took underwater shots, and then was with me when she got there. It was awesome. She brought her own dive suit, but the scuba place had these great ones that are designed for special-occasion diving."

"Special-occasion diving?"

"I know, right?" I painted my big toes. "It seems that it's not all that uncommon for people to get engaged underwater. Anyway, they had this sparkly green and blue suit that made her look like a mermaid. Keith put on this black dive suit that was designed to look like a tux."

"She had to know something was up . . ." Felicity said, her baby blue eyes wide.

"No, I explained that part of the kids' show was a episode about a mermaid scavenger hunt. I told her the segment was called 'Treasures of the Sea.' She bought it. I gave her and Keith the first clue to find the treasure. They went off into the pool and Cesar filmed the whole thing."

"Wait, did Cesar have a dive suit?"

I grinned. "Yes. You know, he didn't look half bad in it, either."

Felicity giggled. It was good to see her happy for the moment. I knew that she was still worried for Warren. He was not in jail—his lawyers had gotten him out within a few hours—but he was inundated by the press. He had spent two hours telling Felicity it was good that we had taken her to Aunt Betty's for a few days. He didn't want her to be followed or badgered. So he had asked her to continue to stay away until things died down.

Seeing how sad and upset Felicity was, my parents had decided that one of us—besides Aunt Betty—should stay with my sister at all times. I told them I was happy to spend the nights if they took the days. All in all, it worked for everyone. I couldn't imagine my parents sleeping in the twin beds. Although my mom told me the secret is to push the two beds together.

"So Cesar got into the pool with them and shot video of them going through the clues." Felicity hugged her pink and white striped pajama covered knees. "How many clues did you have?"

"There were nine clues—one for each of their six-month anniversaries." I continued to put the first coat of polish on all my toenails. Eyeing them critically. "What do you think? Two coats of polish or three?"

"Two," Felicity said. "Please continue the story . . . they followed the clues and . . ."

"And discovered the little treasure chest." I leaned back against the headboard. "I had the scuba company hide it in the deep end close to the sunken ship."

"And? When did he ask her?"

"They brought the waterproof bag to the surface. Then I directed Amy to sit on the edge of the pool and open the bag. She was delighted by the treasure chest."

"And then Keith asked her to marry him . . ."

"Yes." I smiled brightly. "He was still in the water and asked her to open the chest, which she did. Once she saw the blue Tiffany box, she was so surprised. Then I waved for the hotel concierge to open the doors to the ballroom and her family came out to the glass wall to watch and Keith took out the box, opened it to the ring, and popped the question."

"And she said yes!"

I laughed. "Of course she said yes. They kissed and he pulled her back into the water and into his arms."

Felicity sighed. "So romantic . . . not nearly as romantic as mine, but still well done." She clapped.

"Keith's family was so amazed." I checked the polish and it was dry so I grabbed the jar for a second coat. "His father asked me what my normal fees were. So I gave him my card."

"That's awesome."

"Even better." I looked at my sister. "After the proposal we had the engagement party. Keith's family was so happy. His dad wrote me a check." I put down the polish and leaned over the bed to my purse, which was on top of my overnight case. "See?" I pulled the check out and waved it in the air. "My first payment in my new business. He could not believe the amount of thought Keith and I had put into making the engagement a splash."

"And now your new business will make a splash, with thirty percent profit, I hope," Felicity added.

I nodded. "Warren taught me well."

At the sound of Warren's name, Felicity's eyes teared up. "Oh, Pepper, poor Warren! What are we going to do? He's been arrested and has to go to court. I don't see how we could ever celebrate our engagement now."

I got up and hugged my sister. "Don't worry. We'll get this straightened out. I'm certain of it."

"I hope you are right," Felicity said. "I've finally found happiness. I can't lose it now, Pepper. I can't."

Chapter 22

Felicity finally fell asleep, leaving me to stare at the ceiling and listen to her breathing. I was still humming from the success of my first paying event.

I went over everything that had happened from start to finish. Gage had really come through with the movie props. I don't know what I would have done if I hadn't had the sunken ship and the other things I'd rented.

My heart warmed at the memory of standing with Gage and watching the workmen together. I thought about what he said about breaking up with Emma and I realized that I was happy he'd broken up with her.

That thought made me sit up. What? I was happy Gage wasn't dating Emma? No, no, I was happy he wasn't dating anyone. I hugged my knees and remembered how good he smelled. How nice it was to share my ideas with him. How he'd been so interested in everything, while Bobby never cared about anything I did that didn't have something to do with him. Even then Bobby just usually complained about everything anyway.

Gage, on the other hand, always complimented me . . . Wait! Was he attracted to me? Was that why he was so upset when I said I'd help him get back together with his girlfriend? I hit my forehead with my palm. "Stupid, stupid!"

Felicity mumbled something at my outburst and rolled onto her side, facing away from me. I fell back into the bed. What if Gage was attracted to me? What if we dated? The idea appealed, but then there was still Bobby. Poor Bobby, who didn't understand that when I said we were over, we were over. I tested the thought instinctively like you worry a painful tooth. The memory of finding out about Bobby cheating on me with Cindy helped me see that I was truly over him. Even sad and sorry Bobby couldn't generate enough pity to make me change my mind. I smiled to the darkness. I really, truly was free.

I flipped onto my stomach. Wait, would it be okay to date Gage with him and Bobby being friends? Ugh. I pulled the pillow over my head. I needed sleep. Surely the whole "Gage attracted to me" thing was only a crazy-can't-sleep thought anyway . . . unless it wasn't.

* * *

The next day the press had moved on to the next big news story. It would be weeks before Warren had his court date.

That gave Warren and his lawyers plenty of time to figure out what to do next.

Felicity and I had said good-bye to Aunt Betty after we finished the breakfast dishes. Then I'd driven my sister over to Warren's apartment.

"There are odd things going on at the airport," Warren said as he poured us coffee. "I don't like it." He handed us thick mugs of the hot brew. Then pulled out a chair and sat down at his kitchen table with us.

Warren's downtown loft was twice the size of a normal apartment. I remember Felicity telling me about it when they first started dating. She had said that Warren had gotten a great deal when the original owner had gone bankrupt. But if you looked very close, Warren's furniture and accessories were all high-end. The kind of expensive antiques that could seem like flea market finds to the untrained eye. Even the mug in my hand matched white dishes I'd seen in a boutique on State Street.

"Things going on at the airport? What kind of things?" I asked. The coffee was good. Now that I knew the real Warren, I could see how he wore his wealth with an effortless comfort.

"I've been looking at the accounting books. There's money missing. Whoever is taking it is good. Only a real accountant would notice."

"Warren loves accounting." Felicity glanced my way. "He's a genius at it."

Felicity only had eyes for Warren. I felt a bit embarrassed that I'd never felt that way about Bobby. Boy, was I a fool.

"Wow, that takes some guts to embezzle in the middle of a police investigation." I tapped my fingers along the porcelain side of my cup.

"Whoever is doing this is good." Warren reached out and took Felicity's hand. "There have been small thefts here and there."

"Like what?" I drew my eyebrows together.

"Things are missing out of luggage. Small but expensive things have disappeared from the hangars. I can't tell if they are doing this in the middle of the investigation due to arrogance or if they are attempting to distract the police with these small incidents."

"You should call Detective Murphy." Felicity pressed her hands to his. "They need to know what's going on."

Warren frowned and shook his head. "I can't. It would look as if I were attempting to influence the case. Besides, my lawyer says I'm not to talk to anyone without him or his partners present. It's too easy for the prosecutor to twist my words."

"I have to agree," I said. "Listen, I've made a few connections at the airport. Let me see what I can find out."

"I'd help you," Warren said. "But I can't be seen anywhere near the investigation."

"Pepper will do it," Felicity said. "Won't you, Pepper?"

"I'll do my best." I patted Warren's arm. "I know Detective Murphy has his own agenda but he seems to really care about finding the truth. If I can find a connection between these thefts and Randy's murder, he'll listen."

"I hope so," Warren said. "I hate having to rely on others to solve my problems."

"But this is not a problem you created," Felicity said.

"Plus we are practically family," I added. "Family helps each other out. Isn't that what you told me?"

Warren shook his head and smiled ruefully. "I am the luckiest man alive."

* * *

I put on my best manners and went to see Detective Murphy. "Hi, Officer Truant," I said as I approached the front desk.

Officer Truant squinted his blue eyes at me. "We had a lock installed on the door to the back," he informed me. "You can't get in unless I push the Open button."

"Okay." I placed the pink bakery box on the counter in front of him. "I came to apologize for my bad behavior."

"What's this?" He eyed the box suspiciously.

"It's assorted treats from Deerfields Bakery—my way of apologizing."

He opened the box with a great deal of caution. I guess I couldn't blame him. I had been a little unreasonable the last time I was in the police station. It was definitely time to change tactics. His face lit up at the sight of the chocolate, chocolate peanut butter, and marshmallow bacon cupcakes.

Then I watched as his expression turned from amazement back to suspicion. "What do you want?"

Okay, so cops didn't bribe as easily as Jimmy. I clasped my hands behind my back. "I would like to see Detective Murphy, please. I want to apologize to him as well."

"You could have called."

I winced. "I really needed to do it in person." I tilted my head. "But I understand if he doesn't want to see me."

Office Truant took the box and put it on the counter beside him. "I'll call him."

"Thank you." I purposely stepped away from the desk. There were a few chairs in the foyer. I sat down in the farthest one. The only way to prove I had changed was to act as if I truly had. Which meant I could not hover over Officer Truant or stand next to the door as if I'd push through at the first opportunity.

I listened as he spoke low. I couldn't tell if what he said was good or bad. Turning my face away from him, I noted how few cars were parked in front of the building. I couldn't imagine they got many visitors here. I glanced back at Officer Truant. His bald head and broad facial features exuded confidence and safety. These men and women dealt with a lot of people in distress. I'm not certain I had appreciated that. Like most people, I took the presence of the police for granted.

Right now, I was happy to know that there were good officers of the law between me and the bad guy.

"You're lucky, Ms. Pomeroy," he said as he hung up. I stood and stepped back up to the desk. "He'll see you." The door buzzed. "Go on back."

"Thank you!" I hurried through the door before he changed his mind.

Detective Murphy sat at his desk doing paperwork. Today he wore a white dress shirt, and a blue and red striped tie. I noted the plain gold band on his finger and for the first time wondered how long he'd been a widower and if he ever took the band off. He must have really loved his wife. I bet they were a great family. I know he'd mentioned how I reminded him of his daughter. I assumed that was a compliment.

"Thanks for seeing me," I said as I approached. Standing, I waited for him to offer me a seat.

"Truant tells me you want to apologize."

I clutched my purse. "I do. May I sit?"

He waved his hand toward the plastic chair next to his desk. I sat and waited for him to look at me. It was disconcerting that he hadn't even looked up since I came into the room.

While I waited, I became aware of my surroundings. There was plenty of activity. The large open room was divided into several cubicles with more than one person per cube. Phones rang. Someone argued in a loud voice while someone else laughed across the room. There was the sound of fax machines and printers. It smelled manly, of stale coffee, aftershave, and hard work—both mental and physical.

There was a row of plastic chairs up against the far wall. Two young boys with baggy pants and oversized shirts leaned back in their chairs looking defiant.

"All right, I'm listening." Detective Murphy put down his pen.

"I'm sorry I stormed in here the other day and yelled at you. I realize you are a busy man with years of experience and I'm only a self-employed event planner. You know far more than I do about investigating murders and the proper procedures of the law."

He studied me for a moment. "And?"

Oh, good lord, he sounded like my father. Thank goodness I had a lifetime of experience at making a proper apology. "I will do my utmost best not to ever do that again."

"Good."

"But I am a redhead and sometimes my emotions get the best of me."

"I know." He lowered his chin and looked at me over his reading glasses. "That's why I had them install the lock on the door."

The heat of a blush pushed up from my chest straight into my cheeks. "Okay. I guess I deserve that. As long as we understand each other, we're good."

"We do." He nodded and sat back. "Is that all, Pepper?"

I tilted my head. "Um, no. I spoke to Warren this morning. He says that there have been thefts at the airport lately."

"I'm aware of the thefts." He nodded.

"He also said he's pretty sure there's been money missing in the accounting books since Randy's murder."

That got Detective Murphy's attention. "How much?"

"I don't know." I shook my head. "Warren didn't want to say until he dug deeper. He did say that whoever is doing it is good at hiding it. It might be a while until he can track it down."

"I've got a forensic accounting staff member," he said. "I'll send them to Mr. Evans if he's really interested in looking into it."

"Thank you, I'll let him know. Do you have a card for this person so Warren can tell his attorney?"

"Yeah." Detective Murphy reached into his desk drawer and pulled out a card. "If he really thinks this is going to help his case, I'd suggest he doesn't drag his feet."

"Thanks." I took the card. "Again, I'm sorry about my past outburst. You see, Warren is the one who suggested I start my Perfect Proposal business. He's been so kind to help me with my business plan and he's offered to be a silent partner." I raised my hand to stop Detective Murphy from speaking. "Before you say anything, I need you to know that I believe Warren is doing it out of kindness and good business sense. I see the way he treats Felicity. He loves her. I simply can't believe someone this kind and caring would murder someone. I don't know what proof you have—"

"And I can't share."

"I understand. I'm simply letting you know that I realize my feelings may have colored my perception of the issues in this case." I stood. "I'll try to be more objective in the future."

Detective Murphy studied me a moment. "I believe you will."

"Have you interviewed everyone who was at the hangar that day? I know you were waiting on a few people who went on vacation."

"Everyone has been interviewed, Pepper, and they all have alibis. That's why we arrested Warren."

"What about the evidence on my tape?" I asked. "Did you check into that?"

Murphy rested his elbows on his desk—his eyebrows pulled together slightly, his mouth flat. "I watched the video, and frankly I didn't see anything suspicious. And—" He interrupted me as I took a breath to argue. "No laws were broken. Besides, the flight attendant's alibi is tight. Pepper, it doesn't make any sense to spend limited resources pursuing imagined possibilities."

He sat back and his chair creaked. "We have a golden rule in police work. If it looks like a duck and quacks like a duck, it's most likely a duck. Do you get my drift?"

"Yes." I swallowed. "Is it okay if I spend my limited resources pursuing possibilities both real and imagined?"

"Let me give you two pieces of advice. One, never ever break the law. It doesn't do anything but make you a criminal. That means breaking and entering and anything else that you know is wrong."

"Okay." I had to work to relax my fingers. I'd clutched my hands together until my knuckles were white.

"Two, let me know the minute you discover anything

criminal in nature. Do you understand? Don't be a hero. If you see a crime, call 911. Deal?"

"Deal, and I promise to let you know the minute I learn anything that has to do with this case without expecting you to act instantly on it. Okay?"

"All right. Have a good day, Pepper."

I knew a dismissal when I heard one. I left the police station with the forensic accountant's card in my purse. It seemed that sweetness really did attract better results than anger.

Chapter 23

☿

"There is no way Laura Snow isn't involved in this," I said to Felicity.

"What are you going to do?" She was back at work and had called me on her break because she knew I'd gone to see Detective Murphy.

"I need to get back in the airport and scope it out. There is something that Daniel Frasier and Laura aren't telling the cops. I can just feel it." I drummed my fingers on my steering wheel.

The car smelled of Bahamas vanilla from the scented beads that hung from my rearview mirror and that particular essence of old car. It was warm as the sunlight reflected off my dash.

"I thought you were working on your next proposal." Felicity's voice crackled through the line.

"I am," I said. "I only now got out of the initial planning meeting. His name is Mike and his girlfriend is Evelyn. She's a librarian and loves the movie *The Mummy*."

"Wait—the original with Boris Karloff?"

"No, no, the remake with Rachel Wiesz—she plays a librarian studying Egyptology. Evelyn said it was the first movie she'd ever seen where they created a sexy librarian."

"How are you going to put that together in a proposal?" Felicity sounded confused.

"I have some ideas but first off I need to visit the Chicago Public Library and see what kind of space I can rent."

"Keep me posted on that," Felicity said. "I need to get back to work."

"I will." I hung up my cell phone and tossed it on the seat beside me. I figured I had three places to go now. Number one, I could go to the public library and scope out the space. Or number two, I could call Gage and invite him over for dinner. Or three, I could go back to the airport and see if I couldn't discover more about Laura and Daniel. After all, it was Daniel who told me about the authorized-personnel space on the plane. Maybe he wanted to ensure I didn't pay attention to the door and who or what may have been behind it. Would there be anything at the airport that would point to Daniel as a killer? It seemed highly unlikely, but I was desperate to figure this out. Desperate enough to go back to the crime scene.

The real question was how could I convince Jeb to let me back inside the airport after that cop had told me to stay away? Jeb'd let me in earlier as long as I promised to bring him any clues I found. But then I hadn't found any clues. Could I tell him I'd learned about the other mysterious crimes at the airport and wanted to look again?

No, I shook my head at that thought. Jeb might kick me out for wasting his time.

A great thought occurred to me and I put the car in gear, backing slowly out of the parking space. I would tell Jimmy and Jeb that I needed to scout out the space for another client's proposal.

If I mentioned renting the space, I might connect with Jeb. Especially if the airport was in a bit of trouble as both Warren and Jeb himself had told me. Jeb would be looking for extra cash.

Satisfied, I drove down Milwaukee Avenue. But not before I stopped at Fresh Farms and picked up a container of six cupcakes. I know Jeb said I was to stop bribing Jimmy, but I hoped that as long as I kept plying him with treats, he'd keep looking out for my best interests.

* * *

"Hey, Miss Pomeroy." Jimmy opened the window on the guard shack. "Back again?"

I smiled my prettiest and batted my eyes. "I just can't keep away from you boys."

"Got any food that needs taste testing?" He peered around me in an attempt to catch a glimpse of the backseat.

"I do. Can I come in?"

"Sure," Jimmy said, "but I'll have to log you in. Jeb was pretty upset that you were nosing around."

"Wait, he told me I could investigate as long as I keep him in the loop."

"Yeah, well, he didn't like the fact that you didn't see him until the second time you were here. So now he wants written record of who comes and goes these days."

"Sure, no problem. I promised him I'd keep him up-to-date if I found anything. I didn't. Now I'm not here to investigate." I told the lie smoothly. "I'm here to look into the possibility of doing more jet proposals."

"Oh." Jimmy's expression was pure disappointment. "I thought you said you needed taste testing."

"Don't worry, I need your help in that aspect as well."

"Cool." Jimmy's smile lit up his face, and he bent down to log me into his entry book. Once he opened the gate, I shot old blue around to the guard shack. Jimmy met me at my parking space, and I handed him the cupcakes as I got out of the car.

"Is that orange chocolate?" Jimmy pointed to the cake with the orange slice on top.

"Yes," I said. "I may be doing an Asian theme. You

know, flying the friendly skies of Japan Air . . . or some such thing."

"Sounds . . . interesting."

"Thanks." I walked with him into the guard shack. There was a new sign-in board tacked to the wall listing employees. I noticed a certain pilot with an X by his name. "Oh, is Daniel here?"

"Yes, he's doing a walk-through on the plane with Laura. They have to carry an executive to Aspen, Colorado, for more than a meeting. It's a two-day party and I think I heard Laura say she wanted to gamble while she was there."

"Huh, they have casinos near Denver?"

"I heard there were several within thirty miles of Denver." He shrugged. "I don't know. I've never been out there, but Laura has. You should ask her."

"Okay, I will, but first I have a question," I said. "I don't know if you know this, but is the compartment at the back of the plane really off-limits?"

"What compartment?" Jimmy looked confused.

"The one in the back."

"Oh, you mean the luggage space?"

"Okay, sure, the luggage space. Is that what goes back there?"

"It's not always used," Jimmy said. "Sometimes we get a ride that wants to bring their entire wardrobe, so it's good to have a place for large bags."

"Daniel said it was authorized personnel only. Do you know why?"

"Got me." He shrugged. "Maybe he didn't want you behind the engines or something."

I frowned. "Then it shouldn't matter if I look at the space or not?"

"Why would you want to look at it?" Jimmy asked.

"Last time I had Cesar hide in the restroom. I think it might be better if he could set up the cameras and then go to another space and monitor them for the right moment."

"Oh, sure, I guess that makes sense. Listen, we implemented this new ID badge rule. I figured you might be back so I made you a badge. That way you won't have to be escorted as a visitor all the time."

Jimmy handed over a badge. It said AUTHORIZED and had my name, PEPPER POMEROY, underneath. "Cool." I flipped it over. It had a female avatar where my picture should be.

"I found a redheaded avatar for you." Jimmy grinned. "I thought you'd appreciate it."

The cartoon character looked like a redheaded Jessica Rabbit. The old movie line went through my mind—*I'm not bad. I'm just drawn that way.* "I do appreciate it," I said sincerely. Hey, he didn't make me look like Olive Oyl. That was a step in the right direction.

"Wear it whenever you're on-site. That way people will know you've been authorized to look around."

"Thanks, Jimmy." I gave him a quick hug and left him to his cupcakes. I got back into old blue and clipped my ID card on the collar of my pink polo shirt. There were people who thought redheads shouldn't wear pink.

Personally, I loved the color and wore it no matter what people thought. Besides it looked good with my fair skin.

I parked along the side of hangar number four and got out. My new badge in plain view, I pulled a notebook and pen out of my fake-alligator-skin tote and made some sketches of the scene. If whoever called the cops on me last time tried that tactic again, I could counter with Jimmy's ID badge. If that was not enough, I could explain that I needed dimensions for possible future proposals.

My actions had to be in line with these backup plans on the off chance that whoever didn't want me at the airport was watching.

I used the camera on my phone and took a few shots to balance out my sketch. Then I opened the side hangar door and entered. "Hello?"

There was no answer. The place was quiet as a tomb and smelled of jet fuel. The plane that Warren had taken to New York sat in the same spot it was in the day he had proposed. The offices were dark.

"Is anyone here?" I called. "Hello?"

No answer. I noticed that the door to the ladies' room was propped open. I poked my head inside the tiny room. It was clean and smelled strongly of bleach. I supposed I'd have a hard time using a toilet that a dead man had been shoved into. I wondered if they would gut it and start over or simply spray it down with disinfectant and pretend nothing had happened.

My experience with men was that they would probably spray it down and pretend it hadn't happen. A small shudder went through me. It might take me a while to use a public restroom again without checking all the stalls first.

I took a couple of photos and moved on down the hall. It was small. There were the side-by-side bathrooms and the hall ended in the door I had come in. Across from the bathrooms were the two offices. I tried to open one but it was locked. The window was dusty, but from what I could tell, the room was used mostly for storage. The second office was the one I had been interviewed in. I knew it well and wondered who actually used it. Was it maintenance or the flight crew?

The door was closed, but I tried it and discovered it wasn't locked. I looked left and then right to see if anyone was watching me enter the room. No one was there. I turned on the light and took a couple more pictures. There was a coat tree, a couple of file cabinets, and the desk and chairs. The desktop held a calendar, a phone, a computer monitor, and a keyboard. I wiggled the mouse, but the computer did not come to life.

Whoever worked in this office had turned off the computer. Or hadn't come in to work yet. I glanced at my watch. It was 2 P.M. It was more likely they worked early and were gone for the day. I heard voices. They sounded familiar. As far as I saw it, I had two choices—to say hello and continue the ruse about planning another proposal, or to turn off the light, close the door, and eavesdrop on the staff.

I'm usually too polite to eavesdrop, but for some

reason, I turned off the office light and closed the door. I supposed I could get in terrible trouble if I got caught. But I was smart. I trusted that I would figure out something to say should they find me in the dark office.

"I told you Warren would not stay in jail," a male voice said. "Out of all of us, he's the one with enough money to hire good lawyers. I bet he doesn't ever even have to go to court."

"It's not Warren that worries me." Laura stood in front of the office window and faced the plane. "This whole thing is awful, just awful." She put her hands over her face, and Daniel stepped in to comfort her.

I shrank back into the shadows as my thoughts churned. Were these two having an affair? I remembered the ring on Daniel's finger. The man was married. Still he was a flirt, and from what Jimmy said, these two worked together a lot. As I watched them now, it wasn't hard to believe they could be having an affair.

Laura snuggled in close and trembled in Daniel's arms. Her shoulders shook and a sob came out. Were they the killers? It was hard for me to believe that Daniel would kill anyone, but clearly Laura had things to hide.

I knew she was married, too, and not to Daniel. Daniel turned his head and looked into the window. My heart raced as I stepped as far into the shadows as possible. Did he see me? I couldn't tell. The lights were such that his eyes were half hidden.

Fear lightninged down my spine. I clutched my notebook to my chest and searched my brain for a reason why

I was in a dark room watching them. I thought I was smart but panic made my mind go blank. Surely Daniel saw me and would storm in and confront me.

My eyes closed in fear. I felt like a rabbit confronted by a fox. Maybe, if I stayed very still, they might not know I was there.

Chapter 24

I stood in the dark for what seemed like forever and waited. If Daniel had seen me, he had not given any clue. But he did take Laura by the elbow and escort her out of the line of sight of my office windows.

Eventually things grew quiet and I eased the door open. If Daniel or Laura was there, I'd have some explaining to do. I stuck my head out the door and noted that the plane's steps were down. There was a light on inside the jet. If they were inside, it was my turn to flee. I closed the door behind me and hurried down the hallway toward the side door.

"Pepper? Is that you?" Laura called from the other side of the plane.

I plastered on a smile and turned to face her. "Hi, Laura," I said and walked toward her.

"Hi, what are you doing here?"

I clutched my notebook. "I have another client interested in a jet proposal for his girl. Warren said I could look around as long as I didn't copy his proposal to Felicity."

"Oh, when did you come in?" She drew her eyebrows together and she tilted her head.

"A few minutes ago." I pointed to the side entrance. "I parked out there when I saw that the hangar door was closed. It's kind of crazy to walk by the crime scene." I visibly shuddered. "How do you do that every day?"

"It's tough," she admitted. I could tell by her expression that my change of subject distracted her. Tears formed in her eyes and I noted that she couldn't look at the now open door.

I stepped in closer. "Did you know Randy well?"

"I saw him almost every day but didn't talk to him much." She shrugged. "We both had our things going on."

"I heard he had money troubles."

Her expression closed. Her mouth went flat. "In this economy there are a lot of people with money troubles."

"Boy, I understand that," I said with a wry smile. "I was downsized in my last job. If it weren't for Warren, I would be worried as well."

That calmed her down a bit. My goal was to get her talking and keep her talking. I suspected that she and Daniel were having an affair, and if I were a betting kind of person, I would bet that Randy found out and tried to blackmail them.

She crossed her arms. "Wait, Warren Evans hired you?"

"Oh, no." I put my hand on her forearm. "He inspired me to start my own business." I pulled out one of my new business cards. "Perfect Proposals, I plan wedding proposals and engagement parties. After I did such a great job for Warren, he sent me to one of his friends. I planned a 'splash'-themed proposal and party. It was great. Anyway, that's why I'm here. My client list is growing and Warren said I could look at the hangar and get some ideas for other events." I leaned in close as if to confide in her. "I think Warren would like it if I drummed up some extra business for the airport."

"Oh, oh right." She relaxed her arms and sent me a small smile. "Do you think that men would rent a private jet for a proposal weekend?"

"Yes," I said. "I do. My clientele is pretty high-end." I put my arm through hers and walked toward the plane. "I understand you work part time as a nurse?"

"EMT," she said. "Warren pays me by the trip. That means that sometimes I work four hours and sometimes he covers an entire weekend. It's like being on call."

"I hope he gives you health insurance."

"Oh, I don't worry about that. My husband Frank's job covers that."

So she was married. "What does Frank do? If you don't mind my asking. I mean, doesn't he hate when you are away for a couple of days?"

She gave me a small smile. "Frank is in business development. So he's gone a lot."

"That must be tough."

"It was at first, but you get used to it."

"Can you show me around the plane again?" I asked. "I would love to kind of sketch out the interior so that I can draft a plan for placing decorations, music, and such for any client who wants to use the plane for their proposal."

"Oh, um, okay." She walked me around the nose of the plane. "Daniel, look, Pepper's here," she called up to the pilot's window and waved her hand when Daniel saw us.

He got up and met us at the gangway. "Hey, Pepper, how's it going?"

"Good, thanks," I said. "Can I come up?"

"She wants to sketch the dimensions of the plane for future events."

"Future events?" Daniel waved me up the stairs. "What kind of events?"

"Pepper started her own business," Laura said behind me. She stood so close I could feel her breath on my neck. It was as if Laura and Daniel had me sandwiched between them. A creepy sensation had me stepping into the main cabin as fast as I could.

My wild imagination suspected that these two could murder me and fly off to dump my body in some unknown area, never to be seen again.

Then I remembered that Jimmy had signed me in, so at the very least my family would know where I last was.

"What kind of business?" Daniel asked as he leaned against the bulkhead.

"I call it Perfect Proposals." I handed him my card. "Warren suggested it. He said, since I did such a good job on his and Felicity's engagement, I should go into business."

"Huh." Daniel looked at the back and the front of my card. "People pay money for that?"

"I certainly hope so." I laughed and took out my notebook. Sketching the interior dimensions of the plane, I noted where the seats were, the bar, and the restroom. I glanced up to see them both watching me closely. "I promise if I have any proposals that involve airplanes, I'm going through Warren. Hopefully we'll be working together a lot."

"More trips would be good." Daniel stuck my card in his pocket. "Isn't that right, Laura?" He winked at her.

I noted that she blushed. From the look in Daniel's eye, there was definitely something going on between them. "Do you two always fly together?"

"We are Warren's flight crew. The thought was that eventually there would be enough traffic to get a second crew and more planes, but for now, it's only us."

"Oh, wait, do you have a job today? Am I interrupting?" I did my best innocent act, tilting my head and batting my lashes. It never worked on my mom and dad, but that didn't mean it couldn't work on somebody else.

"Oh, no, no," Laura reassured me. "We were supposed to take a client to Denver, but he had a last-minute meeting and canceled. That's what happens with these high-powered players."

"He canceled?"

"More like rescheduled," Daniel said. "It's a pain because we have to come back tomorrow and go through the preflight and everything again."

"Oh, that's terrible."

"It's part of the business." Daniel shrugged.

"In fact, I'm only here because I left my gear in the stowaway compartment. I debated leaving it, but thought better. I came back in to get it."

"There's a stowaway compartment? On the plane?"

"Oh, gosh yes," Laura said.

"You called it a stowaway compartment. Have you ever stowed people?" I had to ask. When she glanced at me funny, I thought I covered myself well. "I'm looking for places to stash my videographer besides the bathroom."

"Oh, no, no," Laura said with what looked like relief on her face. "This is to stow away our gear." She opened a thin cupboard in the tiny pantry area. "It would be nearly impossible to put a human being in here, see?"

She opened it up and stuck her arm inside. The cupboard was tall but thin and about eighteen inches deep.

"Maybe if they stood sideways," I said and climbed inside to demonstrate. It was a very tight fit, but I was thin and straight. I stepped out. "Yes, I suppose that wouldn't do to hide Cesar in."

"I think you're stuck with the restroom," Daniel said.

"What about the luggage compartment?" I asked. They

both looked at me as if I were speaking a different language. "You know where you put the luggage . . ." Still only quizzical looks. "That area with the door for authorized personnel only," I pushed. "That's the luggage compartment, right?"

"Right," Daniel finally said.

"There is no way you could put a person in there. It's not pressurized and they would freeze," Laura said. Her voice held a strange tremor.

"Or suffocate," Daniel added. "Not a good idea at all."

"Okay, well, then that clears that up." I turned and continued to sketch dimensions as if I had no idea what had frightened them.

I did indeed have an idea. The way I saw it, they were having a secret affair. Randy, who was always strapped for cash, had found out about it. I mean, they weren't good at hiding it. I found out about it. So a man who was always around cleaning offices and such would have easily known.

If Randy knew, he could have blackmailed them both. I glanced over to see that Laura had gotten her bag and left. Daniel stood by the doorway watching me. I sent him a smile. "I hope I'm not keeping you from your work."

"Oh, you're not," he said, his gaze serious. "I'm trying to figure out what you're thinking."

"Excuse me?" I froze.

"Your perfect proposal plan for the airplane," he said

and crossed his arms. "I'm curious as to what more you can do than you did for Warren."

"Oh." I laughed with relief. "That's the thing. Warren said I could use the plane—in fact, he encouraged me to use it—but he also said I couldn't duplicate what I did for him and my sister." I waved my hand at the now austere interior. "It's why I had to come back and get dimensions and such." I lifted my sketch book. "I purchased this great little program for the computer where you simply put the dimensions of the space in and then you can move things about."

"Interesting," he said.

"Well, I think I have everything that I need for now," I said. "It was good to see you again, Daniel."

"Take care of yourself, Pepper," he said as I brushed by him to leave the plane. "I wouldn't want to see you get hurt."

I paused at the bottom of the steps and looked back at him. "I'm sorry, I didn't catch that."

"I said take care of you," he replied. "It's hard when you find a dead person. Harder still to come back to the place where it happened. Don't let it get to you."

I drew my eyebrows together. "I won't . . . thanks."

I left the building a lot faster than I had entered it. Climbing into my car, I settled my things on the seat beside me. Laura and Jeb were each other's alibis. Was that the plan? Time of death was never exact. Had Laura sought out Jeb to ensure she had an alibi that didn't include Daniel? Daniel had the flight log as his alibi, but logs could be faked. Still that explanation didn't fit with what I knew of Laura and Daniel.

As far as I could see, the two were threatened by Randy, but neither seemed to be the killer type—if there was such a thing. Still, they may have hired a professional. Yes, that made more sense. That way it was no muss, no fuss. They could have flown him in and established their alibis while he did the deed. Then they could have hid him in the plane and flown him back out with no one the wiser.

Now all I had to do was prove it. Maybe there was a way for me to get a look inside the luggage compartment. I could ask Warren if what they said about pressurization and such was true or not. He would know. Wouldn't he?

I frowned. But then I would have to tell him why I was asking and I didn't want to do that yet. I didn't want Warren to worry about me.

And unfortunately, I couldn't take my suspicions to Detective Murphy without some kind of concrete proof. Not if a video wasn't proof enough for him. I sighed.

Then I spotted movement in my rearview mirror. A closer look told me it was Laura. She was talking to someone. I ducked down out of sight far enough that she couldn't see me but I could see her in my side mirror. It was Daniel she spoke to. They kissed and then separated.

Laura turned and got into a gray Toyota. When she pulled out, I started up my car and followed. It was difficult to be inconspicuous. Old blue stood out in a sea of cars as much as I did in a sea of people. It had never been a problem before. Now when I wanted to tail someone, it was nearly impossible to be incognito.

Thankfully Jimmy stopped me at the gate. "Hey, Pepper, learn anything new for me to report to Jeb?"

"No, nothing new. I did, however, get some dimensions of the plane for my next jet proposal. Thanks for that. Tell Jeb I will keep him posted."

"Okay, will do." Jimmy opened the gate and let me out. I could make out Laura's gray Toyota in the distance. Since Jimmy had stopped me, there was no way for her to suspect I was following her.

I did my best to keep three cars behind her. When she turned down a side street, I kept going, turning onto the next street. I went around three blocks then doubled back.

Laura had parked her car in front of a brick row house. I made a sudden decision and pulled up to the curb. Maybe, just maybe, if I confronted her like the reporters did sometimes on television, I could surprise a confession out of her.

"Pepper, what are you doing?" Laura asked as I got out of the car.

"I followed you," I admitted. "Well, then I went around the block a couple of times." Okay, I was an awkward interviewer. Good thing I wasn't trying out for the local investigative news.

"Why?"

"I have to know, are you and Daniel having an affair?"

Laura's head snapped back as if I had slapped her. "What? What gave you that idea?"

"I saw you kissing good-bye. Aren't you both married to other people?"

"I'm not having an affair with Daniel," she protested and put her hand on her chest, flashing her wedding ring. "I'm married."

"So is he, but I saw you kissing," I pointed out. "And I know that you both had motive to get rid of Randy. All told, that seems pretty suspicious to me, Laura, I'm not going to lie." I put my hands on my hips.

"What's suspicious?" Laura glanced around. "Wait! Are you thinking we had something to do with Randy's murder?"

"You and Daniel have pretty tight alibis. Too tight, if you ask me. Most people don't know where they were at any exact time of day, let alone ensuring they were with someone," I said. "Most are like Warren; they go about their day not worried about alibis. And I know that Warren Evans didn't do it."

"How do you know? Are you Warren's alibi?" she asked, drawing her brows together in a frown.

"No," I said. "I know Warren and he wouldn't kill anyone. I need to prove that for my sister's sake. It makes a difference to Warren's case if you two are having an affair and plotting alibis. Don't you think that's the tiniest bit suspicious?"

She took me by the arm and drew me toward her

house. "Please come inside. I don't want to talk about this where my neighbors can hear."

I followed her into the home.

"Can I get you something to drink?"

"Sure," I said.

"Ice tea okay?"

"That would be wonderful." She left toward what I assumed was the kitchen. The inside of the brick row house was warmly decorated with tan paint on the walls and blue accent colors. It had been remodeled recently, and white crown molding gave the room a rich look. There were several pieces of art including original oil paintings.

"Wow, these are beautiful," I said as I stared at the pictures. "They look like originals."

"Yes, Frank loves his art." She set a tray of ice tea glasses, sugar, and a bowl of lemon wedges down on the dark cherry coffee table. "My husband does very well for himself."

"But he's gone a great deal, isn't he?" I added a slice of lemon to my tea.

"I want you to know that Daniel and I are good friends," Laura said. "But we would never alibi each other. I can't afford to lie and have my husband find out."

"Why is that?"

She sat up with concern on her face. "Frank would divorce me in a second." She looked down at her hands in embarrassment. "You see, I have a gambling addiction."

"Wait, what?" I leaned forward. "I thought Randy had a gambling addiction."

"I don't know if Randy had an addiction or not." She shrugged and sipped her tea. "But I do know that I have a problem. I've driven my family to the brink of bankruptcy twice. It got really bad. I kept lying about it until the bank calls and the credit reports couldn't be hidden. Both times, Frank managed to bail us out." She took a deep breath and let it out slowly. "If he even suspects I'm lying about something, I'm gone."

"And Daniel?"

"We're friends," she insisted.

I sipped my tea. "How many people know about your money problems?"

"Only a few." She leaned back. "Why?"

"It would make it very easy to blackmail you," I pointed out. I searched her face for any telltale sign of distress. I noted that her left eye ticked a bit, but her expression seemed frozen. In a second she smiled brightly . . . too brightly.

"Oh, no one would blackmail me. I work with the best people." She laughed but it held a fake tone. "Imagine anyone trying to blackmail me. They all know I have no money. I'm working two jobs for goodness' sake."

I leaned back and tried to hide my frown. "Of course, of course, everyone knows you have no money. I do have one last question . . ."

"All right, I'm an open book."

"Who was in the back of the plane?"

"Excuse me?"

"I want to prove Warren didn't do it. The only way to

prove it to the police is to be able to point out who was in the hangar at the time of the murder. I saw you talking to someone that day. I'm thinking they were behind the authorized-personnel door. Do you remember who that was?"

She frowned in thought. "As far as I know, there was no one behind that door. Are you sure you remember me talking to someone?"

"I'm pretty sure . . . but I suppose I could be mistaken."

"Maybe you're thinking of when I put the luggage near the compartment. Daniel loaded it on the plane, not me."

"And you don't remember talking to anyone near there?"

"Oh, gosh, no. I don't remember even seeing anyone back there. But I'll let you know the minute I think of it. Is that okay?"

"Thanks, you've been a big help."

"Well, I'm certainly glad you followed me home and we got this straightened out," Laura said a bit too cheerily. "I would hate to have you following clues that simply aren't there. It would be like a dog chasing her tail. Don't you think?"

"I suppose." I blew out a long sigh. "I'm positive Warren is being framed."

"Oh, I don't know about that." She wiggled back into her couch. "They have to be pretty certain before they arrest someone. Especially someone as socially connected as Warren Evans."

"Mistakes happen all the time." I looked her in the eye and put my glass down. "Someone framed Warren. They want to throw the cops off their trail and they're using Warren to do it. I intend to find out who that is and get the detectives back on the right track and away from Warren."

"Good luck with that," Laura said. "And good luck with your new business."

"Thanks." I stood and handed her one of my business cards. "If you know anyone who wants a special event for their engagement, please pass my card on to them. Especially if they want a plane event. That way I can drum up extra work for you and Daniel."

She rose and took my card. "Thanks, I will." We walked to the door. "Can I give you a word of advice?"

I turned in the door frame. "Sure."

"Let the police investigate Randy's murder. The system is pretty good, you know. If Warren is innocent, then he'll be fine. If not, then the right person has already been arrested and Randy is avenged."

I said nothing but smiled at her and went back to my car. It was warm inside old blue and I noted that Laura watched me like a hawk. Time to go. I'd think things through later.

I pulled away from the curb and gave her a little wave. She waved back, but stayed at her door. I turned back onto the highway.

Her explanation made sense . . . so why did I still think she was hiding something?

Maybe it was her poor acting skills. Or maybe I was really barking up the wrong tree. There was one way to find out for sure—talk to Daniel. I could usually tell when a man was lying—well, except for Bobby. It was a family trait that my mother had passed down to me.

It was why Warren's lie of omission bothered me so much. I should have known right away.

I wove through traffic. Maybe my sense of right and wrong was messed up, or maybe, just maybe, there was more going on at that little airport than I had ever imagined.

Chapter 25

"Bobby, what are you doing here?" I stepped up to find him hanging around my apartment door. He loomed large in the antique white-painted hallway.

"Hi, Pepper." He straightened. "How have you been?"

"I'm fine. What do you want?" I had my keys in my hand but didn't want to open my door. I didn't want Bobby back in my apartment ever. It's not that I was angry with him. It was simply that we had been together so long it would be easy to fall back into the habit of having him in my life.

After seeing how happy Felicity was with Warren, I didn't want to settle for habit. I wanted a real relationship with a man who cared about me. A man who listened to me. A man who wanted to help me. A man who would go to the ends of the earth to make me happy.

Looking at Bobby, I knew he was not that man. He'd had years to prove otherwise.

"I miss you, Pepper," he said and shoved his hands in his jeans pockets. He wore a jacket with a dark T-shirt under it.

"Oh, I don't think it's me you miss, Bobby," I said softly. "I think it's the habit of having me around."

"You're wrong," he said quietly. "I'm sorry I smarted off the other night. I should have given you a real proposal . . . like that Warren guy did."

"It wouldn't have mattered." I put my hand on his biceps. "We aren't in love."

"How can you say that?" he asked, his brown eyes sad as a puppy. I bit the inside of my check to keep from falling for his sadness. "We spent years together. You are my one true love."

"No, Bobby." I crossed my arms. "I'm your first date, not your true love. It's a habit is all. Why don't you go out and meet another girl. One whom you are crazy about."

"That's just it. I'm crazy about you, Pepper." He took my hand in both of his. "What can I do to prove it to you?"

"Too late. If you were truly crazy about me, you wouldn't have been cheating on me with Cindy Anderson. Men in love do not cheat."

"She didn't mean anything to me."

I tilted my head and looked at him closely. "Bobby,

there simply aren't any fireworks between us. Do you even remember what I was talking about before you said, and I quote, 'I suppose this means you expect me to propose to you'?"

He winced at his own words. "Listen, I was drunk."

"That's not exactly a good thing, is it?" I frowned. "You get drunk a lot, Bobby. It makes you so unhappy."

"I am unhappy." He shrugged. "I'm miserable without you in my life."

"You were miserable with me in your life. Go home, Bobby," I said. "Take care of yourself. Figure out what makes you happy and then go get it." I patted his arm. "See you around."

I unlocked my door and closed it quickly behind me, making sure to lock the dead bolt. I stepped away from the door and the image of him moping in front of it. This was best, I told myself. I'd wasted years of my life hoping he'd love me. If we were truly right for each other, I'd know it by now.

When I said "love," I meant real love. The kind of love I'd seen between Keith and Amy, and Felicity and Warren. The kind of love my parents had. The kind where if they spent one day apart, they were miserable.

Bobby and I had been broken up two weeks now, and besides having to remember not to say "I love you" when I said good-bye, there really wasn't anything I missed.

I went to the stove and turned on the tea kettle. I took out a porcelain mug and one of my favorite herbal teas.

I had a lot to think about. Bobby was, for once, the least important on my list.

* * *

"Hi, Gage." I stopped by the prop house to look at new furnishings and try to drum up ideas for Mike's proposal.

"Hey, Pepper." Gage's face lit up. "Good to see you."

"It's nice to see you as well. Listen, I want to thank you for helping make Keith's proposal so great."

"It's not a problem, really." Gage stepped up close. I could smell his cologne on his warm skin. He wore a blue dress shirt with the collar open and the sleeves rolled up. Even though he had a warehouse and rows of dusty props, Gage always dressed like a professional. His pants were pressed and his shoes clean. His pretty blue eyes sparkled.

"Listen, this time I need some things for this guy named Mike Moorehouse and his girlfriend, Juliet."

"No problem." Gage smiled. "What kind of things?"

"This one has an Eastern theme. They recently took a trip to China. She fell in love with the décor while he fell in love with her." I put my hands around Gage's arm and walked toward the warehouse door. "He wants an opulent and over-the-top proposal. Best of all, Mike has a budget of twenty-five thousand dollars. So I need your best props and I will pay your best prices."

"Ah, Pepper, you know I'd loan them to you for free."

"Gage, you are in the prop business and I have a customer who can pay. Let's see what you have."

"Okay, come on to the back." He drew me toward the far left corner of the warehouse. "These are things from a movie that was filmed downtown a few years ago. What's your venue?"

"I'm renting the top deck of the Willis Tower," I said. "Mike wants them to literally be on top of the world."

"Cool," Gage said. "Let me show you a few things. You pick out what you like and I'll have my guys deliver, set up, and tear down."

The warehouse was nearly a block long and two stories high. The floor was concrete and there were rows and rows of wide, sturdy shelves crammed with everything from a giant stuffed bear to dining room sets to chairs and dishes. It was a decorator's dream. Most of the things were used only a few times and then stored for years.

The building echoed with the beeps of a forklift and rattled in the wind. It smelled of concrete, dust, and old fabric.

In the back corner were three sets of wide shelves with wood platforms and steel legs. They were filled with assorted bits of pottery and chandeliers and bling.

"Let's dig through these and see if you like anything."

"You are the best," I said and admired his bottom while he climbed a stepladder to the second and third shelves.

He handed down three four-foot-tall vases made of the finest porcelain and hand painted with romantic Chinese scenes such as a boat on a lake and cherry blossoms.

"What else do you have?" I asked.

"Working on it." He popped his head over the top of the shelf. "I've got a komodo dragon with gold-trimmed toenails."

"It sounds awesome. Hand it down."

We spent two hours together combing the warehouse for pieces to go in the ballroom at the top of the Willis Tower. I eventually picked out the best pieces to be set aside and took photos of them with my phone. Later I would download the photos along with the dimensions and place them inside the computer 3-D picture. Once I was happy with the design, I'd send pictures of the entire space to Mike for his final approval.

"Have you heard from Bobby lately?" Gage asked as I snapped pictures.

"Yeah, he showed up at my door yesterday," I said as I moved around the pieces to change angles. "He thinks he misses me."

"Do you miss him?" Gage asked.

"You know . . ." I winced, put my arms down, and turned toward Gage. "I don't miss him." I blew out a long breath. "That sounds horrible, doesn't it? Don't get me wrong . . . I miss the idea of him, but frankly, Gage, I don't miss Bobby. I know you are his best friend, but—"

He put his hand up to stop me. "Don't ever feel as if you can't tell me something, Pepper," Gage said. "Yes, Bobby's my best friend, and I know you two broke up . . ."

"You were there," I said. "Wasn't that the most awful thing ever?"

He shook his head. "I don't blame you one bit. I don't

want you to ever feel as if you need to spare me because Bobby and I are friends. I know what a jerk he can be sometimes. I was surprised you stayed with him as long as you did."

I sent him a wry smile. "I guess I kept hoping that the high school football star would fall in love with me. I can see now that simply because I wanted it doesn't mean it would happen."

"Are you still in love with him?" Gage's tone went soft. "The high school football star?"

"Oh, gosh no," I said and shook my head. "That's the thing. I think I was more in love with the idea of having a quarterback for a boyfriend than I was in love with Bobby."

Gage was quiet for a moment.

I took two more pictures. "How's it going with Emma?" I asked and tried not to look at Gage. "Did you get back together?"

"No." His tone was brisk. "I never wanted to get back together with her. You see, unlike Bobby, I knew I didn't love her."

"Oh." I turned toward him slowly. "So you're single like me."

"Yes." He nodded and shoved his hands in his back pockets. "I'm single, like you."

"Funny how things work out, isn't it?" I stood frozen to the spot. My phone dangled from my fingertips.

"Yes, it is." He took a step toward me.

"Is it hard for you to work with me since you are Bobby's best friend?"

He drew his brows together and his mouth tightened. "What do you mean?"

I shrugged. "Girls don't date their friend's exes. It's like an unwritten rule. In fact, a real friend will bad-mouth him more than I do." I tilted my head. "Don't guys do that? Or are you still friends with me so that Bobby can keep tabs?"

Gage laughed; it was a loud and hardy sound. "Men do not worry about that kind of thing . . ." He grew sober. "Well, at least I don't. Listen, Pepper, I've known you since grade school. You broke up with Bobby, not me. I would never snub you because of your choice to date or not date Bobby."

"That's a relief." I blew my bangs out of my face. "I know that I would miss you."

That was about the biggest hint I was ready to give the guy.

His smile grew and he took another step toward me. "I would never abandon you, Pepper. You can't get rid of me as easy as Bobby."

"Oh," I said and stared up into his beautiful gaze. He caressed my arms with his thumbs, sending a shiver up my spine. "Thanks."

"You're welcome." He dipped his head and kissed me. I was thrilled to discover that Gage was as good a kisser as he was a friend. I put my arms around his neck and stepped in closer. He smelled of cologne with a hint of hard work under his starched shirt.

I leaned in to the kiss and felt the excitement clear down to my toes.

He pulled away just about the time I was ready to go deeper.

"What?" I asked, trying to hide my disappointment.

"I'm not sorry I kissed you."

"Oh, well, neither am I." I took a step back. "But there's still the problem of Bobby."

"What about him?" Gage asked. "You broke up with him, right?"

"Right," I said seriously. "But I don't want to cause you to lose your best friend."

"Don't worry, Pepper." He brushed the hair out of my eyes. "I'm a big guy capable of making my own decisions."

Chapter 26

♂

"What about a zeppelin?" Mike asked me. "To keep with the opulent, out-of-this-world theme of my engagement. Is it possible to get a zeppelin to dock off the Willis and carry us away to our hotel destination?"

"A zeppelin?" I repeated. Do they have zeppelins in the United States? Well, there was the one they used to televise golf and other sporting events. "I'll see what I can do. Keep in mind there are flight regulations around the buildings in town."

"I know you can make it happen, Pepper." Mike's voice was sincere through my cell phone. "Remember, money is no object. If you have to grease a few palms, simply say the word and I can get it done."

"Got it." I hung up the phone. Where the heck would

I get a zeppelin, and what kind of permits would I need to have it dock at the Willis? I assumed it could dock wherever a helicopter would be able to land. I had no idea if that was a safe assumption or not. Who would know about zeppelins?

Jimmy might know, or Jeb or even Laura for that matter. If she was still talking to me after I suspected her of murder.

I drove up to the airport gate. Jimmy waved me through and I parked near the guard shack. Luckily, I had picked up a dozen donuts earlier. It never hurt to keep bribing my guy on the inside.

Besides, if Laura didn't do it, then I still didn't know how to help Warren. It wouldn't hurt to do a bit more snooping under the guise of asking questions about zeppelins and their docking regulations.

"Hey, Pepper, what do you have that you need tasted today?" Jimmy opened the guard shack door. Today he wore jeans and a uniform shirt embroidered with the word SECURITY and his name.

"I don't need anything tasted," I said as I wiggled out of old blue.

"Oh." His shoulders slumped and his mouth curved down.

"But I did bring my favorite security team some donuts." I pulled the bakery box out of the car. He was beside me in a moment.

I was wearing a shift dress. I figured it never hurt to show a little leg when I needed information. No, that was a lie. To be honest, I was hoping I'd run into Gage. I couldn't get last night's kiss out of my mind.

"Wow, jelly filled." Jimmy's face lit up. "Come on in. I have coffee."

"Thanks, Jimmy," I said. "I don't need coffee." I followed him into the shack. "Do you know if there is anyone in the area that rents a zeppelin?"

"A zeppelin? What is that?" He had already gone through two donuts by the time I sat down.

"You know that big balloon-like thing that floats over parades and golf tournaments and such."

"Oh, huh, I never really thought about a zeppelin . . ." He shoved a third donut into his mouth and spoke with his mouth full. "You should talk to Jeb. If anyone knows the air scene around Chicago, it's Jeb."

"Great." I stood. "Is he in this morning?"

"Yeah, I think he's in the main office." Jimmy looked down at the remaining donuts. "Did you want to take him a donut?"

"No, you keep them," I said. "Thanks, Jimmy."

"Hey," he called after me.

"What?"

"Don't forget to sign in." He held the door open for me with one hand and clutched the donut box with the other.

"Oh, right, thanks." I went inside, signed the log book, and picked up my ID badge. "Thanks, Jimmy."

"No problem," he said from his perch on the stool with his mouth full of donuts.

Jeb was sitting at his desk when I knocked on his office

door. His muscular form appeared bulkier than usual. His hair was freshly cut in the military manner he preferred. He exuded intimidation as easily as I exuded awkwardness.

"Come on in, Pepper," Jeb said without looking up.

"Hi, Jeb, Jimmy said you might know the answer to my question."

He looked up as I took a seat in one of the chairs in front of his desk. "What can I do for you?" His dark eyes were sincere under bushy brows.

"I have a client who wants to get a zeppelin to dock at the Willis and carry him and his gal away after the proposal. Do you know where I can rent one?"

"Ha!" Jeb laughed and then leaned forward. "Seriously?"

"Seriously," I said. "Do they even have one around here? If so, where can I find it?"

"Of course they have them. This is Chicago. There are all kinds of events here where the blimp is involved in filming." He wrote down a name and number on a piece of paper. "Here's the name of a friend of mine. Call him. He'll help you out."

I took the paper. He had written down the name *Brian Bradford*. The phone number had a Chicago area code. "Thank you. Can I tell him you sent me?"

"Sure." Jeb leaned back and put his hands behind his head. "How's the murder investigation going?"

"I don't know, you tell me." I played it cool.

"Oh, come on, we both know you don't think Warren

did it. Then I saw you poking around here the other day and you didn't come see me and keep me in the loop—like you promised."

"Oh, no, I wasn't investigating," I sat up straight and worked hard to calm the blush that always came when I fibbed. "I was scoping the place out for future proposal events. I'm sure I told you that I started my own small business, Perfect Proposals." I handed him my card. "It was Warren's idea."

He studied the card. "What did Laura Snow have to do with a proposal event?"

"Laura?" I drew my eyebrows together.

"I saw you two talking."

"Oh, yes, I asked her to give me a tour of the plane so that I could figure out where to hide the videographer."

"I see." Jeb put down my card. "That was it?"

"Sure, why?"

"I could have sworn you followed her out of the gate. Do you suspect her of something?"

I froze. "Um, no?" Then I smiled. "I mean, what would it matter if I did? The cops have their suspect. The last thing they would do is listen to an event planner."

"Right," he said. His smile turned bland. "I told you that I like to keep tabs on the comings and goings around the airport. You promised me you'd keep me in the loop if you discovered anything."

"Yes, I remember and I told Jimmy on my way out that I didn't learn anything. Didn't he tell you?"

"He gave me some story, but then again he didn't see you talking to Laura." Jeb eyed me. "I found it suspicious that you both left at the same time."

"You keep tabs on when I leave?"

"It's my job." He crossed his thick arms.

"You wouldn't know anything about a cop who stopped me as I left the airport the other day, would you?" I watched him closely to see if my question surprised him. Unfortunately the man had a solid poker face.

"Why would I?"

I shrugged. "It's interesting that you watch me leave because you think I'm acting suspiciously and then a cop stops me and tells me an employee at the airport called in the description of my car as suspicious."

He raised one bushy eyebrow. "Were you acting suspiciously?"

"No. I told him you said I could look around. Then he fined me fifty dollars for a taillight being out."

"Was it?"

"Was what?"

"Your taillight, was it out?"

"Yes, but that's not the point." I waved my hand as if to dismiss the idea. "You've trusted me with my own security badge. Why would I act suspiciously and keep something important from you if it meant losing my privileges?"

"Indeed, why would you risk losing your privileges?"

"I wouldn't."

He studied me, his gaze unwavering. I concentrated

on the space between his eyes. "Fine. I had to ask. It's my job as head of security."

"I completely understand," I relaxed.

Jeb nodded at me and then smiled. For a moment I got the impression his smile was predatory. But then it turned genuine.

"Call Brian. He can hook you up with a zeppelin guy."

"Thanks, Jeb." I left him in his office. Strange how Jeb had noticed my following Laura. If he paid that close attention to the comings and goings at the airport, how did he miss a murder right under his nose?

It was something to think about. Stepping outside, I figured that while I was at the airport, I should stop and see if Daniel was about. It was high time I asked him a few questions. I left old blue at the guard shack and walked over to hangar four. The airport was small but there was some traffic. A Learjet took off in the distance. Someone drove a limousine up to hangar five. A truck loaded things onto a plane in hangar six.

I went into the side door and called out, "Daniel?"

"In here," I heard a male voice say from the office. I went in to find him on the computer. "Hey, hi, I was in talking to Jeb and I thought I'd see if you were around."

He pushed the keyboard aside and put the full force of his blue gaze on me. He grinned. "Hello, Pepper, you look wonderful."

I patted my windblown hair down. "Thanks." It took work not to protest, but Felicity had told me I needed to do better at taking a compliment. "How have you been?"

"I'm good."

"I went to see Laura the other day," I led into my story. "Did she tell you?"

He grinned. "Yeah, she said that you thought we were having an affair. That was an interesting idea. I have to say, though, as pretty as Laura is, I do love my wife."

He put his elbow on the table and rested his chin on his fist.

"So you're a big flirt is all," I teased him.

"Only when a woman is as pretty as you."

I widened my eyes and blushed hot. "Can I ask you a question or two about the night Randy died?"

"Ask away, doll."

"Was there anyone in the luggage compartment? You know, the part of the plane you told me was for authorized personnel only?"

"Was there anyone in the luggage compartment? Like who? Who do you imagine would be in the luggage compartment? If he flew away with us, then he's probably dead, and if he's dead, then the smell would be overwhelming . . . I imagine."

"I don't know who. That's why I'm asking you. I saw Laura talking to someone while she stood next to the compartment door. If there was someone else in the hangar at the time of the murder, the police need to know it."

He tilted his head and studied me a moment. "I was in the luggage compartment. I loaded the luggage. Normally Ralph, the plane mechanic and all-around guy on the go, would do it. But he was on vacation that day."

"Ralph was on vacation. How come I haven't heard of Ralph before?"

"There's no reason for you to have heard of him," Daniel said. "He wasn't there. He was with his wife on a cruise. I'm sure the cops already checked that angle."

I blushed harder. "I'm not checking angles."

He gave me the eye.

"Okay, I might be checking angles, but only because Warren is innocent. I just know it."

He reached out and took my hand in his. "You seem so sincere. I wish I could help you. The truth is I like Warren and was shocked by his arrest. If I knew anything that could help you, I'd tell you. Okay?"

"Okay." I got up. "Thanks, Daniel."

"Anytime, doll." He went back to his computer.

The only thing left to do now was to concentrate on my business and call the zeppelin guy Jeb had told me about. Helping to prove Warren's innocence would have to wait.

Chapter 27

♂

I took old blue out into the countryside. The suburbs were considered country if you lived in the city, but this, this was real rural Illinois. Complete with flat prairie, cornfields, and cows.

The zeppelin didn't pan out, but the guy Jeb sent me to knew a guy who flew a biplane. I had him set up a meeting to discuss the use of the plane. If it were in my budget, I would consider using it for Felicity's engagement party as well. A biplane would be a great addition to a *Great Gatsby*–themed event.

But first I had to convince Mike that a biplane was better for his proposal. Once I'd done that, I'd look into hiring a wing walker. How cool would that be for Felicity's party? Maybe even have them write a message in the sky.

I knew Mike would like the idea of "Will you marry me?" written across the sky. It didn't get much more opulent than that.

I was tasked with checking out the plane, gathering details and photos, and getting back to Mike. If this panned out, there would be an extra five-hundred-dollar bonus in it for me that I could use as my gift for Felicity and Warren's party. I really wanted this to work out.

I checked my GPS one more time as I careened down the winding two-lane highway. "In one half mile, your destination is on the left," the machine told me. "Your destination is on the left."

Spotting a long driveway, I turned off the road and down a dirt two-track that ran between two rows of pecan trees that were enormous and, therefore, very old.

The dirt track ended about three-quarters of a mile from the highway. I parked old blue and got out. I grabbed up my camera and studied the sky. It was bright blue with wisps of puffy clouds. That special autumn blue that meant the sky above was cold. I wondered if the pilot would have to wear a down flight jacket as he flew or if cold weather mattered to old biplanes.

The plane was parked under a tarp that stood next to a large oak tree in what looked like a cow pasture. I snapped a couple of pictures from that distance. The pilot/owner had given me permission to look around the plane, even hop in if I liked. I approached it with caution.

Unlike the jet, this plane had a front propeller so I knew to stay away from the front end. I snooped around a bit, amazed that they could simply leave a plane out in the open like that. This one was tan with chrome trim and a polished wood dashboard. The seats were leather. I opened the pilot side door and peered in. It was not like a car at all. There was a steering wheel and some kind of sticks to shift, but I wouldn't have any idea what to do.

I looked around. The pilot, a Mr. Hank Menturm, owned the farm and had built his own runway. In the distance was a big barn and I imagined that he housed the biplane in there. He'd gotten it out for me, of course, and it rested at the very end of the mowed runway.

The wings were long and held together with strong cables. I tugged on them and tried to picture someone climbing out of the backseat and onto the wings to do tricks. One quick glance around told me I was alone, so I hopped up on the wing and pretended to walk it. The wing surface was tilted as the tail was down and the nose was up, but I held on to the cables and climbed around.

It struck me that it would be fun to take a picture of me on the wing. I could then Photoshop out the ground and make it look as if I were actually on the wing in flight.

In my trunk was a tripod I had just bought so I could interview prospective brides' families. Having the interviews recorded would allow me to go back and watch them when I was stuck for ideas. A glance at my watch told me that I had at least twenty minutes before the pilot arrived. So I hopped down and strode back to my car.

I grabbed the tripod and spotted a large gold trophy

prop Gage had left behind at the splash event. I grabbed both and headed toward the plane. In a flash I had the camera set up to take video. Then I climbed up on the wing and pretended to wing walk, showing off my trophy at the end. I waved and blew kisses to my adoring public.

"Hello, Pepper." Jeb appeared from behind a stand of trees to the right of the runway.

"Oh!" I put my hand on my heart as embarrassment rushed through me. "You startled me. I didn't know anyone was here."

He sauntered over to the camera and pulled it from the tripod. "Go ahead, wave. I'll take a still shot."

My heart pounded in my chest at getting caught walking on the wing. The last thing I needed was photographic proof of the moment. "Um, no, no, that's okay. I shouldn't be up here." I scrambled down off the wing with the trophy in my hand.

Jeb was beside me when I turned around. "You have a bad habit of being places you shouldn't." The tone of his voice sent shivers along my spine.

"I'm sorry?" He was getting even closer, so I put my hand out and touched his chest in a clear message to stop. "Back off. You're scaring me."

"That's funny. I've been trying to scare you for weeks and you simply didn't get it. Now all I have to do is get close to you to scare you?"

"What do you mean? Why are you acting this way?" I tried to scoot by him, but he had me trapped up against a cable.

"I know I saw you follow Laura out the gate the other day. Why did you do that?"

I shrugged. "I suspected Laura and Daniel might be having an affair."

"So?"

"So." I swallowed hard. "Randy could have found out about it and been blackmailing them. Even Jimmy knew Randy was a regular at the casino. Everyone knew he needed money."

"So you confronted Laura, even after they arrested Warren Evans?"

"I told you. I have to know the truth. My sister's future depends on it. Besides, I can't imagine Warren killing anyone. Can you?"

"Evans?" He let out a dangerous laugh. "No, no I can't imagine him doing the deed. A guy like Evans is too soft."

The look in Jeb's eyes scared me, and I realized that we were quite alone and a long way from anyone that could help me. I clutched the handle of the metal trophy I held behind my back. "But you could do it, couldn't you, Jeb?" I whispered. "You could kill Randy."

"What did Laura tell you?" His eyes had a dark color to them. His brows drew down and he looked dangerous. His mouth was a thin line. I swear he radiated displeasure.

"She didn't tell me anything." I held on to that trophy like it was a life preserver. He stood too close. If I brought it up now, he could deflect it or take it from me. I stepped toward him and he instinctively took a step back. It was enough to give me room to maneuver around the cables so that my back was no longer against the wing.

"Liar!" He grabbed my arm and shook me. "You were in her house a very long time. What did she tell you?"

"How do you know how long I was in her house?" I answered his anger with anger. It was either that or tears and I refused to let a bully see me with tears.

"I followed you out that day, you little snoop. I knew I couldn't trust women and you two proved it. She told you, didn't she, about her not-so-little gambling problem." His voice grew silky. His breath was hot against my face.

"She told me her husband bailed her out twice," I agreed. "She also told me everyone knew she didn't have money so there was no way anyone—not even Randy—would try to extort money from her."

"Did she tell you she was desperate? Did she tell you that she just couldn't help herself and had gotten into financial trouble a third time?"

"No." I shook my head. "No, besides she's still with her husband. He would have kicked her out had she gotten into trouble again. She told me so herself."

"That's why she came to me for help," Jeb said. "Oh, she tried Daniel first, but that guy's all talk and no action. He laughed her away."

"But you didn't, did you?"

"No, I didn't. I've been watching her for months, flirting and carrying on with Daniel, a married guy. She never once gave me the time of day."

"Until the day she was desperate for money . . ."

"She came to me in tears," he said. "She told me Evans wouldn't help her because he was too good a friend to her husband. He would tell on her for sure. She rubbed up against me and led me right to my checkbook."

"You bailed her out knowing she couldn't repay you?" I took a step back. "But it wasn't money you wanted. Was it?"

"No, it wasn't money. She knew it then. She teased and promised until she cashed the check."

"Then she refused you?"

"The tease wouldn't go through with the affair. I took to reminding her on a daily basis."

"You stalked her."

"I reminded her of our bargain." Jeb's face grew dark. "The bitch thought she could handle me. *Me?!* As if I'm some stupid jock."

"She couldn't handle you, could she, Jeb?"

His gaze turned hard. "She thought she was so smart. She took adrenaline from that nursing home she works for and lured me into the ladies' room."

"She was going to kill you?" That was hard to imagine . . . Laura killing Jeb. "She had to have been terribly desperate."

"She didn't have the guts to kill anyone," Jeb spat. "She threatened me with the syringe but I called her bluff. I had her up against the wall so fast she didn't know what hit her." He took a step closer and I took a step back. I could hear his breathing speed up at the memory. "I got the syringe out of her hand when that damned janitor came busting in."

"You killed Randy."

"Damned right. He threatened me with the mop. I reacted as any combat veteran would. I swung. I forgot about the syringe until it landed between Randy's neck and collarbone. It only took a second before I pushed the plunger."

"He dropped to the ground." I finished the tale.

Jeb's eyes glittered. "I had Laura good then. You see, she was the one with the syringe. The stuff came from her workplace."

"It would be your word against hers and who wouldn't believe you? A war vet? A good guy . . ."

"The security chief." Jeb's smile was predatory. "Oh, I had her all right. She knew it, too."

"If she went to the police, she would look guiltier than you."

"Right."

I took another step backward, gauging how far a distance I needed to swing the trophy with enough force to earn me some time to get away. "Whose idea was it to frame Warren?"

"Does it matter?" he asked. "Either way I win. I had that woman right where I wanted her . . . until you came sniffing around."

"That's why you were helping me."

"I had to keep an eye on you. Women tend to talk to

each other, trust each other. I couldn't have you believing her . . . falling for her innocent act."

It was then I knew how very naive I was. "You knew there wasn't a zeppelin," I said. "You got the man on the phone to invite me out here, didn't you?"

"A little too smart, a little too late." He grabbed my left arm.

I swung with the right and managed to bounce the trophy off his shoulder. I didn't knock him out or even hurt him. But the blow was enough to startle him and get him to let me go for a moment.

A moment was all I needed. I scrambled, moving toward him instead of away, and scooted under his arms as he reached for me. Good thing I'd dressed for the country today. My athletic shoes dug into the ground, giving my panic traction. My jeans and pale blue T-shirt were not so tight as to restrict me while I ran.

The problem was that I had no idea where I was going. Jeb was between me and old blue, and besides, I could never remember which pocket I put my keys in and would have to stop to figure out how to get them out of my pocket. All this went rushing through my brain as I realized I had dropped my trophy.

A single glance back told me that Jeb was better at thinking on his feet than I was. He had the trophy in his hands as he rushed toward me. I screamed and sped up. Now was not the time to wish I had spent more time at the gym.

I made a beeline toward the big barn/hangar. I needed

a moment to think. To plot. To plan. The only way I could give myself a moment was to find a place to hide.

"There's nothing in that barn to save you," Jeb said behind me. The darn man didn't even sound winded. "You're just prolonging the inevitable."

My thoughts turn crazy when I'm scared. Maybe he was right. Maybe I should stop and kick him or something. Right, like that would save me. My heart pounded in my chest. My lungs strained. All he'd have to do was keep chasing me until I keeled over in exhaustion. There'd be no way they could prove I'd been murdered.

Something near the tree line caught my eye. Was that a person? I veered off, suddenly changing paths toward the movement. It meant that for a split second I actually got closer to Jeb, thank goodness his arrogance and my random running caused him to pause.

It was long enough for me to once again get ahead of him. "*Helllp!* Please somebody!" I shouted as best I could with no wind in my lungs. Okay, throwing up was not an option. I kept running.

I pumped my arms and raced. Don't fall, don't fall, don't fall. In the movies the girl always falls. I was not going to be that girl.

The motion near the trees grew more distinct. It was a man. Please let him be a good man and not the plane's owner.

"Brian, grab her," Jeb called behind me.

"Got her, boss." A stocky sandy-haired man stepped out of the shadows.

"No!" I said and zigzagged past him, cutting up the tree line back toward my car. My phone was inside old blue. If I could get in and lock the doors . . .

I grabbed the door handle as Jeb reached out and slammed his hand on the door. Struggling, I couldn't get past the weight of him against the door. If I got out of this alive, I was going to add weight lifting to my new workout routine.

"You can't kill me." I turned and faced him. "Everyone will know it was you."

"Who will know?" He raised an eyebrow. "Brian? He works for me. Laura? No, Laura won't talk. She has too much to lose."

"Warren will figure it out."

Jeb laughed. "That man can't even prove his own innocence—there is no way he'd prove my guilt. There is no one to link me to you. Besides." His eyes gleamed with hatred. "I have a nice tidy stash of cash. Once your case goes cold, I plan on getting all I can from Laura and hitting the road."

"Felicity knows where I am," I blurted out as my phone rang inside the car. "Plus I have my phone GPS on. They will track me here and you will get caught."

"It's a chance I'm willing to take," Jeb said. He grabbed my arm and dragged me away from my car.

Kicking and screaming and biting, I didn't make it easy for him. He cuffed me upside the head and I saw stars. "Tie her up," he ordered Brian as he handed me off to the fair-haired man. Brian was not much taller than me but he was solidly built. His hands were like iron grips on my arms as he pushed me to the ground and made quick work of tying my hands behind my back.

Having never been tied up before, I can tell you it wasn't what I'd expected. The rope rubbed my wrists raw. The knot was impossible to get to. He grabbed my arm and lifted me to my feet.

"Put her in your trunk," Jeb said. "We'll take her to the quarry."

"You going to kill her first?" Brian's eyes sparked.

"No, then we'd have cadaver dogs poking around your car. She's going to go in nice and alive. We'll kill her when we get to the quarry and toss her over the side."

"Sounds good!"

"No!" I shouted and Jeb hit me again. This time hard enough for my teeth to rattle. I might have bitten my tongue because I heard a crunch. I fell to the ground like deadweight. If they were going to take me away, then they'd have to really lug me. I made myself as unmovable as possible.

"I think you killed her," I heard Brian say.

"Naw, she's still breathing. Pick her up and put her in your trunk."

"Damn, she's heavy." Brian tried to lift me and couldn't. It was hard not to complain when he dropped me. I had to clench my teeth to keep from uttering a sound.

"She can't be that heavy; look how skinny she is."

"So now you're insulting my strength. I'll have you know I can bench a hundred and thirty."

"Then you can lift a stupid girl."

"This girl is a lot heavier than a hundred and thirty."

"Hey." I sat up, offended. "I only weigh a hundred and twenty pounds. That's skinny for five feet eight inches."

"Shit, she's awake." Brian jumped back, startled by my outburst.

"Good. Now she can climb into the trunk herself." Jeb reached down and grabbed me by the arm.

"No." I dropped. He had a hold of my arm and it kept me from hitting the dirt. Brian grabbed my other arm and together they dragged me to the car. I went kicking and screaming.

"Get in the trunk."

"No."

"Put her in the trunk."

"I can't . . . she's kicking." I bit Brian when he reached down to yank me up. "Ow!" He jumped back. "This chick is too much work. Kill her already. I'll douse the car with bleach."

"Fine." Jeb took a small container out of his pocket. He unzipped it and pulled out a syringe. "A little too much insulin and she'll be out for life."

"Hold it right there!" Officer Vandall walked around the corner of a tree with his gun raised. "Police. Put your hands up."

I don't know about you, but when a man with a gun tells me to put my hands up, I generally obey. The problem was that this time my hands were tied behind me.

"Oh, thank goodness," I said and showed my tied hands. "These two tried to kill me."

"Oh, hell," Brian said. "I'm not taking the fall for this." He dropped his hands and took off running.

"Stop!" Officer Vandall wavered. It was enough to make Jeb split off and run in another direction.

I sat with my hands tied behind me, but up as far as I could hold them, which wasn't very far considering the position I was in. The officer said something foul under his breath and took off after Jeb.

"Stop! Police!" Officer O'Riley had his gun pointed at me.

"My hands are up," I said. "You might want to go apprehend someone who's not already tied up." I pointed toward Brian. It was Officer O'Riley's turn to curse. He took off in the direction Brian ran.

I sat for a whole three breaths waiting to see if any other policemen came out of the bushes. When no one did, I wiggled my bum and feet through my arms so that my hands were now in front of me. Can I say, thank goodness for yoga class? I stood and walked toward old blue. The police had things in hand, right? No need to run if I didn't have to.

Pop, pop, pop went gunfire in the distance. It had to be one of the officers. I mean, I'm pretty sure neither Jeb nor Brian had a gun on him. On second thought, I wasn't going to stick around and find out.

My heart beat picked up, pounding loudly in my chest. I ran. Digging the keys out of my pocket wasn't as hard as I thought it might be. I jumped into old blue, locked the doors, and started my car up. Driving was tough with your hands tied together, but I was getting out of there. I had a pretty strong fight-or-flight instinct, and now that my fight was over, flight took hold.

I peeled out of the meadow and onto the two-track drive, passing the single cop car in the lane. "I sure hope they called for backup." Glancing at my cell phone on the passenger seat, I figured I'd call 911 as soon as I got just a little farther away from all the shooting.

I pulled out onto the road as three cop cars came screaming past. Their sirens wailed. I watched in my rearview mirror as they turned and bounced wildly down the two-track. Old blue sped up down the road. If more bullets were going to fly, I didn't want to be anywhere nearby.

Detective Murphy's blue sedan cut me off. I hit my brakes and pulled to the side of the road.

Shoving the gearshift into park, I left the car running, but rolled my window down. Hard to do when both hands are tied together and the window was not automatic. Detective Murphy approached my car with his gun in hand.

"It's only me," I said as firmly as I could and stuck my tied hands outside.

"You okay, Pepper?" Detective Murphy eyed me first, and then peered inside the back window.

"I've been better," I replied. I waited as he walked

around the car and finally put his gun in the holster and opened the driver's side door.

"Did they hurt you?" Detective Murphy asked. He examined the raw red welts on my wrists and then the rough rope.

"How do you know it was a 'they'?" I asked as the radio in his car squawked out the news that both men were in custody.

"We've been following you and Jeb for a while," he said and pulled a pocket knife out and sawed at the rope.

It came off with a yank and I instinctively did what everyone does on television when they are freed. I rubbed my wrists. The problem with that was that they hurt. A lot. I winced.

"There's a first aid kit in my car," Detective Murphy said. "Unless you want me to call an ambulance."

"I think the first aid kit would be fine." I got out of old blue. I knew I was a mental mess when I realized that he reached behind me and turned the car off and pulled the key out of the ignition.

"Come on." Detective Murphy took my elbow and walked me to his car. He opened the door and I sat in the passenger side. Then he went to the trunk, and came back with a tidy white box marked FIRST AID.

He worked efficiently, opening the kit, finding some antibiotic cream and gently smearing it on my raw wrists. I closed my eyes and tried not to cry. I had been scared—really scared. I didn't know how to admit this to anyone.

Least of all Detective Murphy. He had warned me to leave the snooping to him.

"I suppose you're going to say I told you so," I said. My voice was weak and tired.

"Not necessary at this point." He wrapped my wrists in gauze and taped them up. I opened my eyes. "I am going to need a statement." He put the bandages and tape back into his neat kit and closed it. "We usually do that on scene."

"Okay." I closed my eyes again. "I came out here looking to hire a biplane for my next proposal event." I opened one eye. "It's going to be an opulent kind of affair. The guy wanted a zeppelin, but they're hard to find unless you own a tire-manufacturing facility."

"Go on . . ."

"I got here a little over an hour ago. The guy on the phone—he said his name was Brian—said he would be running late, but he gave me directions and permission to come out and look at the plane. I didn't think anything of it." Tears filled my eyes and rolled down my cheeks. "It was all a setup."

"Here." Detective Murphy handed me a tissue. "Then what happened?"

I told the rest of the story quickly and flatly with as little embellishment as possible. "The next thing I knew, I was driving off as fast as I could. I had to get away. If you hadn't stopped me, I might still be driving."

"Someone would have stopped you." His voice was calm.

"Wait. If you had been watching me, then you knew that Jeb set me up."

"We suspected, but there is little we can do until something illegal happens." Office Murphy's eyes were hidden behind mirrored sunglasses. His mouth was a grim line.

"Wait. You mean you had to wait for Jeb to kill me before you could act?" That was insane. I thought policemen were like the cavalry—supposed to come riding up in time to save the damsel in distress.

"It would not have come to that. O'Riley and Vandall never let you out of their sight. They were on strict orders."

Why did that not make me feel better? "How long have they been following me?"

"Ever since you left the airport with a taillight out."

"You mean that officer who gave me a ticket . . ."

"Was sent out to delay you long enough to get our guys on your tail."

"That ticket cost me fifty dollars."

"It's against the law to have a taillight out." Detective Murphy shrugged. His right eyebrow twitched. "Who can I call to come get you?"

"I'm fine. I can drive."

"No, you can't," he said firmly. "You are in shock, and when that wears off, you'll be exhausted. I can't put you behind the wheel. Who can I call?"

I gave him Gage's number. If he called my parents, the phone call alone might give my dad a heart attack. The drive here would give my mom a stroke.

After he called Gage, Detective Murphy got a phone call. "Good. Keep her there until I can interview her." He hung up his phone. "Laura Snow wants to confess everything."

"You know she was only trying to protect herself from Jeb," I said.

"The woman has an addiction problem that needs to be addressed," Detective Murphy said, his tone brisk. "She'll be facing multiple charges from stealing insulin to covering up the murder."

For a brief moment I felt sorry for Laura, but then Gage pulled up and all thoughts of Laura left my head. He got out of his blue hybrid SUV. The next thing I knew, I was running to him. He grabbed me up and held me tight. It felt too good to be in his arms, tears streaking down my cheeks.

Trust me—when I cry, I don't get that pretty movie star crying face. No, I get the red blotchy skin, runny nose, ugly kind of cry. To Gage's credit, he didn't look away. "Are you okay?"

"Yes." I nodded, but refused to take my arms down from around his neck. He didn't seem to mind. His strong, capable hands held me close.

"What the hell happened?" he growled at Detective Murphy.

"We caught the killers," I said with pride in between tears.

"She was never in any real danger," Detective Murphy said. "It took time to call in backup."

"She's shivering." Gage ran his hands up and down my back.

"It's shock," Detective Murphy said. "That's why I called you. We'll have someone drive her car home. I'd feel better if someone else took care of her tonight."

"I'll see her home," Gage said. "Come on, Pepper."

"Wait!" I turned to Detective Murphy. "My camera . . . I left my camera and tripod and one of Gage's props out there."

"We'll see that your things are returned," Detective Murphy said. "Go home, Pepper. You've done enough."

"I solved a crime," I said.

"Yes," Detective Murphy said. "You did."

My knees buckled and Gage caught me. I let him help me into his car and drive away. I closed my eyes and smiled. Warren would be cleared, and Felicity would never have to worry again.

Chapter 28

The engagement party was a huge hit. Warren and Felicity were dressed in 1920s black-tie fashion. My sister was stunning in a pale champagne sparkly gown. They looked like a couple straight out of old Hollywood.

I managed to find a full-length gown in dark green satin. The halter top added curves to my frame. I did my hair up in a twist and had fake pearls cascading down my back.

There were one hundred and fifty guests. Warren's mother met with my mother on two occasions, and they worked together to hone the guest list—each promising to keep the wedding guest list down to three hundred of their closest friends and family.

For the first time in my life, I was happy not to be

planning the wedding. It's not that Warren's family wasn't wonderful. It's just that each mother had her own idea of how to please her child. I could see why Warren liked my mother so much. She was a lot like his, which meant they were either going to get along like gangbusters or they were going to butt heads every step of the way.

My vote was that they would butt heads. But then that was all part of building a new family. Everyone had their expectations, and compromise was the name of the game. Like how I worked within Mom and Dad's budget, but then let Warren pay for extras—such as the part of the venue that wasn't in their budget to make the engagement party something to remember—even if there wasn't a biplane or skywriting.

After what happened with Jeb in the field, I didn't want a reminder of my near-death experience to put a cloud over Felicity's party. As for Mike's perfect proposal, I did find an actual zeppelin. The permits to fly it in town were in the works and the company promised they could run a private message across the balloon.

Unfortunately my five-hundred-dollar bonus from Mike would come too late for Felicity's party. So my gift to them was clearing Warren's name. I would wait for the wedding to get them something special.

"The party is fantastic," Mom said, "like a fairy tale." Mom wore a long gown with bits of red beaded fringe that glittered from the bodice. Her arms were bare, but she made up for it with over-the-elbow gloves in soft red velvet.

"You did all this on our budget?" My dad wore a black rented tuxedo cut in the 1920s fashion with baggie pants and wide shoulders. He had white spats on his shoes. He snagged a small glass of sauvignon blanc and a skewer of grilled scallops with seaweed. We were currently on the second course of the *Great Gatsby* theme of mini wines and crudités.

"You've seen the bills," I said with my fingers crossed behind my back. Of course, they were bills made up just for my dad. The hotel understood when I asked them to split the billing, and having Warren on the same charity board as the president and CEO of the W helped a lot with their cooperation.

"You are a wonder." Mom kissed my cheek and hugged me. "I couldn't be prouder of my girls."

At that moment Warren grabbed a glass of wine and tapped it with a spoon so it rang out. "Attention . . . attention everyone," he said loud enough for the talking to die down. The string quartet paused in their playing. "Thank you. I'd like to welcome everyone here tonight. Thank you for coming and celebrating our engagement."

He hugged Felicity and everyone clapped and cheered as he planted a kiss on her lips then straightened. "Before we go any further, I want to thank my soon-to-be sister, Pepper Pomeroy. Pepper, come up here." Warren held out his hand.

Embarrassment washed over me as I took his hand and let him pull me to the middle of the crowd.

"This lovely woman is the reason we are able to

celebrate tonight." He tugged me in between him and Felicity. "Without Pepper's work, this party would never have happened. Not only did she plan the proposal, but she planned and executed tonight's party."

The crowd of friends and family cheered.

Felicity put up her hands to quiet everyone down. "She is also responsible for risking her life to uncover the true murderer of Randy Stromer and clearing Warren's name. We owe her more than we can ever repay her." Felicity glowed and my heart soared.

"To Pepper Pomeroy." Warren raised his wineglass. "All success and happiness."

"To Pepper," my father shouted out.

"To Pepper," everyone responded and raised their glass. "To Perfect Proposals," I said and raised my glass.

"Here, here," Warren added, and we toasted the happiness my new business created.

Warren's mother, Helen, joined my parents, and the circle of our family was complete. That is what I call good party planning.

Don't you think?

Menu for
Felicity's Engagement Party

Course 1

TUNA TARTARE ON TOAST / RIESLING

Course 2

GRILLED SCALLOPS WITH SEAWEED /
SAUVIGNON BLANC

Course 3

SAUTÉED FOIE GRAS ON CRACKERS /
SAUTERNE

Course 4

GAZPACHO CONSOMMÉ IN SIPPING CUPS /
VIOGNIER

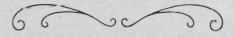

Course 5

LOBSTER ON SKEWER / CHARDONNAY

Course 6

FISH BITES / PINOT NOIR

Course 7

BREAST OF CHICKEN À LA ROSE / CABERNET

Course 8

CHEESES ON PICKS / WHITE RED PORT WINE

Course 9

VENETIAN ICE CREAM CUPS / MONTBAZILLAC

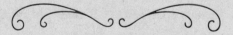

From *New York Times* Bestselling Author

LAURA CHILDS

STEEPED IN EVIL

· *A Tea Shop Mystery* ·

Indigo Tea Shop owner Theodosia Browning is called in
to solve a murder at an upscale Charleston winery after
a body is found in a wine barrel.

They say *in vino veritas*, but everyone at the winery
seems to be lying through their teeth. It may look like
the killer has her over a barrel, but cracking tough cases
is vintage Theodosia Browning.

PRAISE FOR THE SERIES

"A love letter to Charleston, tea, and fine living."
—*Kirkus Reviews*

"Murder suits [Laura Childs] to a tea."
—*St. Paul (MN) Pioneer Press*

laurachilds.com
facebook.com/TheCrimeSceneBooks
penguin.com

M1385T0913

The Tea Shop Mysteries by
New York Times Bestselling Author
Laura Childs

DEATH BY DARJEELING
GUNPOWDER GREEN
SHADES OF EARL GREY
THE ENGLISH BREAKFAST MURDER
THE JASMINE MOON MURDER
CHAMOMILE MOURNING
BLOOD ORANGE BREWING
DRAGONWELL DEAD
THE SILVER NEEDLE MURDER
OOLONG DEAD
THE TEABERRY STRANGLER
SCONES & BONES
AGONY OF THE LEAVES
SWEET TEA REVENGE
STEEPED IN EVIL

"A delightful series."
—*The Mystery Reader*

"Murder suits [Laura Childs] to a Tea."
—*St. Paul Pioneer Press*

laurachilds.com
penguin.com

M314AS0913

WELL-CRAFTED MYSTERIES
FROM BERKLEY PRIME CRIME

- **Earlene Fowler** Don't miss these Agatha Award–winning quilting mysteries featuring Benni Harper.

- **Monica Ferris** These *USA Today* bestselling Needle-craft Mysteries include free knitting patterns.

- **Laura Childs** Her Scrapbooking Mysteries offer tips to satisfy the most die-hard crafters.

- **Maggie Sefton** These popular Knitting Mysteries come with knitting patterns and recipes.

- **Lucy Lawrence** These brilliant Decoupage Mysteries involve cutouts, glue, and varnish.

- **Elizabeth Lynn Casey** The Southern Sewing Circle Mysteries are filled with friends, southern charm—and murder.

M5G0610